WIZARDRY & WILD ROMANCE
A STUDY OF EPIC FANTASY

monkeybrain, inc.

WIZARDRY

& WILD ROMANCE

A STUDY OF EPIC FANTASY

MICHAEL
MOORCOCK

INTRODUCTION
BY
CHINA MIÉVILLE

AFTERWORD
BY
JEFF VANDERMEER

Wizardry & Wild Romance:
a study of epic fantasy

A MonkeyBrain Publication
www.monkeybrainbooks.com

MonkeyBrain, Inc.
P.O. Box 200126
Austin, TX 78720
info@monkeybrainbooks.com

ISBN: 1-932265-07-4

Printed in the United States of America

A Note on the Text

Trajan and Parkinson Cover Fonts, courtesy of
Adobe Systems and the Font Bureau, respectively.

For Jim Cawthorn
who introduced me to so many good writers and whose illustrations over the past forty years have given me so much pleasure
and inspiration…

And for Brian Tawn, Pete Knifton, Dave Britton, Charles Partington,
John Coulthart and other discriminating readers of fantastic fiction
who will continue to disagree with a fair amount of the arguments in
this essay…

And to the memory of
Bill Butler, who died in
his sleep, aged 43, 20th
October, 1977.

CONTENTS

And you love take my right hand,
Come join the faery folks' last dance;
Then we'll sleep and dream of Elfland,
Her wizardry and wild romance.

Wheldrake,
The Elvish Rune,
1877

MICHAEL MOORCOCK – EXTREME LIBRARIAN
INTRODUCTION BY CHINA MIÉVILLE

This book is too interesting. By which I mean:

There is something in the very excellence of *Wizardry & Wild Romance* which creates a frustration in the reader. Reading Michael Moorcock's history of literary fantasy is like walking an immense, brilliantly stocked library, through which you don't know the way, following a librarian who walks briskly, nodding and pointing at various books as he goes.

"Very interesting that one," he says, and "Ah, some good things in there," and you're desperate to stop and examine the volumes, the authors you at best half-recognise or vaguely recall, but your custodian walks too quickly, and you can only stare back at them as you run to keep up. By which I mean:

How can Moorcock possibly write all the books he writes, when he also reads all the books he obviously reads? How?

But no matter that there's a frustration at times, and that you want to stop by a shelf and find out a little more about Henry Treece, or Abraham Merritt, or whoever it is, you can't possibly be grudging, because this is a function of the book's strength: Moorcock's easy erudition. Erudition without pomposity isn't an easy thing to manage, and we have it here. Moorcock is opinionated, certainly: pompous, no.

It's the unusual route itself through the library that's so exciting, such an illumination. So much fantasy fiction has degenerated to the limitless repetition of cliché, the content as degraded as we would expect from copies of copies of copies, that it is sometimes hard to see it as a living form. Fantasy, one could easily believe, is dead, but – as any quick look to publishing schedules makes clear – it doesn't *know* it's dead. It rises out of the mulch of tropes and staggers back to the bookshop. Good god, are we doomed to read a zombie literature?

Well no, as Moorcock points out. It's not only that in this updated edition he has revised his suggestions for further reading, his generous recommendations of others' recent work: it is his consideration of the history itself that reinvigorates the field. It is not only exciting but intellectually liberating to be shown a different route through fantasy's lineage than that we might imagine.

And with the facility of the best pamphleteers, Moorcock makes his counterintuitive comparisons. Why should the basest pulp not rub shoulders, not be *informed by* mediaeval romance, or the resurgent Gothic? Why on earth not? Depicted as he does, these lineages make perfect sense, and our quietly rotting field is exciting again. Not undead after all – a little beaten up, maybe, is all. Nothing that can't be fixed.

There is so much *stuff* in *W&WR*, there are plenty of claims to agree and disagree with. I am strongly with Moorcock, for example, that M. John Harrison is one of the great counterfantasists of the field and a crucial inspiration, or that Alan Garner writes rings around C. S. Lewis. On the other hand, I think he's a bit harsh on H. P. Lovecraft, whose psychotically baroque ramblings disobey all rules of style, true, but still have *something* astonishing, even if it's impossible to say quite what.

But then, of course, the disagreement not only doesn't matter, it's rather the point. Enjoying the argument is much of the pleasure of an opinionated history. As a reader, you're happy to disagree, so long as you feel you're in safe hands. Here the questions of respect and seriousness are key. Though Moorcock proclaims his predilection for some ironies and for fantasy that is not afraid of humour, he comes into his own with a caustic denunciation of a particular lazy kind of "irony."

Irony is one of the great middlebrow palliatives of late modernity. Wankers are no longer shame-faced to buy top-shelf mags because of the great proliferation of "ironic" porn-chic. The resurgence of a new sexism is ok because, y'know, "it's just a joke." The viral triumph of what the two-bit theorist would call "postmodernism." Evidenced at a more nebulous level by the tedious proliferation of films and books that wink enthusiastically over the top of their pages or screens, anxious to let their readers or viewers know that they *know* they're not real, that we're all too too clever to actually *fall* for any of this, so the best thing we can do is get on with being pleased with ourselves for *getting* it all.

There have been theorists and traducers of this impoverished tradition: Lautréamont "scorn[s] and execrate[s] ... an irony employed to extinguish and which displaces precision of thought"; Walter Benjamin denounces "know-all irony [that] makes a great display of its poverty and turns the yawning emptiness into a celebration." Moorcock joins these greats with his brilliant excoriation of "the joke which specifically indicates to the reader that the story is not really 'true' ... [t]he laboured irony ... of the pulp hero or heroine, this deadly levity in the face of genuine experience ... to make the experience described comfortingly unreal."

Moorcock is an unflinching enemy of such deadening, banal knowingness. What he wants instead, and what he introduces us to the history of, is passion, and vision.

Of course, lumpen irony isn't the only enemy of vision and passion. Another is mollycoddling. Consolation, comfort food.

There is, as some of us have discovered, an easy controversialism to be had by simply dissing Ol' Man Tolkien. It's slightly discomfiting. No matter how heartfelt your objections to *The Lord of the Rings* might be, the mere fact of stating them enters you into a kind of performative mode, and you're a tired, too-old *enfant terrible* cranking out the iconoclasm as a party turn. Perhaps it's antipathy – understandable antipathy – to that sense of showboating which leads to such passionate denunciation of Tolkien-criticism (as, in the words of one online commentator, the product of "diseased minds"). And it is this which makes "Epic Pooh" the keystone of this book.

It is a *tremendous* piece of work, in which Moorcock tears apart Tolkien, his style and his legacy, but with a calm authority that isn't oily with radical chic. Instead, Moorcock not only condemns but contextualises, explaining what is wrong, why it's wrong, and where the wrongness comes from. Sure, it's not going to convince everyone. But for some of us who read Tolkien and came away ill at ease, with the sense that we had missed something (Was it our fault? Why did we not love this book? Why, in fact, did it make us feel somewhat queasy?), this essay was an absolute revelation. It was to me. It is one of the pieces of writing which represents a hinge-point in my life. To read something that somebody else has written and have it make better sense of your own reactions than you have been able to, is a momentous thing.

Always political, polemical, with disdain for received opinions and second-hand thinking, with a passionate love of the field and a merciless eye for its failings, with radical opinions and old school precision, *Wizardry & Wild Romance* is a classic, perhaps an anti-classic, of fantasy. It is scandalous when it goes out of print, and a matter of immense satisfaction when it comes back in. Long may it remain so.

We accept too little from our fantastic. We have become much too easily pleased. *Wizardry & Wild Romance* demands something more of us than we are used to giving, an engaged reading, a counterintuition, and in so doing it helps us demand more of the literature we love. Out of respect for Moorcock politics, it seems apt to end with an anarchist, Errico Malatesta. "Everything depends," he said, "on what people are capable of wanting." Fantasy literature is hardly a pressing political priority. But still, in a small and crucial way, we should be capable of wanting more than we get from the fantastic, that, after all, we love. We should be capable of demanding vision, and passion. The things that *Wizardry & Wild Romance* insists on.

FOREWORD

Hobbes, in order to daunt the reader from objecting to his friend Davenant's want of invention, says of these fabulous creations in general, in his letter prefixed to the poems of Gondibert, that "impenetrable armours, enchanted castles, invulnerable bodies, iron men, flying horses, and a thousand other such things, are easily feigned by them that dare." These are girds at Spenser and Ariosto. But, with leave of Hobbes (who translated Homer as if on purpose to show what execrable verses could be written by a philosopher), enchanted castles and flying horses are not easily feigned, as Ariosto and Spenser feigned them; and that just makes all the difference.
Leigh Hunt, *Imagination and Fancy*, 1844

I have no intention in this book of "defining" the term epic fantasy. Neither do I expect my polemics to convince anyone already opposed to my points of view. In general I intend to discuss the subject of romantic fantasy (with the obvious exception of that modern commercial corruption describing a sentimental love story) and specifically touch on an area of fabulous romance whose writers invent their own Earthly histories and geographies. Romantic fiction (especially that by South American allegorists and English post-modernists) is currently enjoying something of a vogue. It is again accepted as a reasonably serious form by our literary establishments. Indeed some academics are prepared to go to excited lengths to discuss the enduring qualities of Tolkien or Rowling.

Until relatively recent times most European fiction originally contained strong romantic elements until it began to be thought unseemly for rational middle class readers to enjoy them, unless in one or two acceptable forms, such as the modern detective story. It's probably fair to say that the rift between romanticism and realism began to manifest itself in the mid-19th century when the novel of manners or the character novel rose to fashionable ascendancy, though the late 19th century founders of the Oxford English school (Walter Raleigh) and the Cambridge school (Quiller Couch) were themselves wonderfully catholic in their own enthusiasms. While Jane Austen established our taste for the subtle social novel, it took F. R. Leavis to insist that moralistic realism was the only serious form of fiction. While literary tastes have again become somewhat more catholic and coined approving terms like "magic realism" we are still haunted by the more old-fashioned school of criticism with which I grew up and which believes fantasy to be not quite kosher. Perhaps the most important turning point in England came recently when Philip Pullman's excellent children's science fantasy series received the Whitbread prize for fiction. In spite of the frank support of such fine social novelists as Elizabeth Bowen or Angus Wilson through the 1950s and 1960s, we only recently began to remember that all the great 19th century realists introduced strong strands of romance into their work and some of them, notably Flaubert with *Salammbo* and Meredith with *The Shaving of Shagpat*, produced gorgeous works of full-blooded and fantastic invention. Since that time it seems that almost every realist has had at least one romance or imaginative satire in them, from Henry James (*The Turn of the Screw*) to Toni Morrison (*Beloved*). The gradual return to academic acceptance of romantic methods has allowed novelists previously accepted as realists to revive themselves with fantasies, parables, symbols, allegories and whatnot, often with disastrous effects. Fashionable middle-brow literary writers, like Martin Amis, A.S. Byatt and many others have injected naïve fantastic elements into their work, suggesting that a new school is emerging of *would-be* Romantics, desperately striving to discover fresh sensibilities in the way repressed products of the middle-classes tried to loosen up with drugs and sentimental egalitarianism in the sixties. These people learned the school rules too well, however, and the main impression given by their fabulations is of red elbows and other miscellaneous bits of anatomy poking out through holes they have, with much effort and personal discomfort, rubbed in the straitjacket. They have, of course, discovered a ready audience in the readership which earlier believed them to be reporting the real world.

I must admit that my own taste is primarily for the likes of George Eliot, Meredith, and Conrad, while Henry Green is probably the modernist I most admire. Ronald Firbank aside, Elizabeth Bowen, Elizabeth Taylor, Angus Wilson, Alan Wall and similar novelists are those I prefer for regular reading, but I still enjoy and respect a good romance if it has wit as well as epic elements and if the characters are not too "distanced." Again the science fantasy best characterised by Pullman and exemplified by what people are calling the new New Wave (China Miéville, Jeffrey Ford, Jeff VanderMeer, K. J. Bishop for instance) is what I prefer. I've no admiration at all for the rafts of Robert E. Howard and J. R. R. Tolkien imitations presently feeding commercial genre demands and will not deal with them here in any detail. I might as well add that I'm also chronically unable to enjoy most good formula fiction, be it by Ian M. Banks, Ian McEwen or Ian Rankin. I prefer the riskier fiction of Iain Sinclair, Tim Etchells, Alan Warner and Steve Aylett, of Stuart Home, Tony White and the school which takes pulp fiction as its chief inspiration. Sadly, I have been able to read almost no epic fantasy since the first draft of this essay was prepared in the late 1970s, just as I am almost entirely incapable of reading so-called "hard" science fiction, though I accept that excellent work is currently being done.

Epic fantasy can be seen as a late development of that element of the Romantic Revival that began in 1762 with the publication of Macpherson's "Ossian" cycle, was continued through Walpole's *Castle of Otranto* (1764) and Percy's *Reliques of Ancient English Poetry* (1765), Chatterton's *Rowley Poems* (1777), the *Lyrical Ballads* (1798) of Coleridge and Wordsworth, Scott's *Lay of the Last Minstrel* (1805), Tennyson's *Poems* (1842), given further impetus by Carlyle's translations and studies of the German Romanticists (such as Burger, Tieck, Hoffman, Musäus, but also Goethe and Schiller) and his books like *Past and Present* (1843) which was to have such an evident influence on the Pre-Raphaelites, through Rossetti (*The Germ*, 1850), Ruskin (*The Stones of Venice*, 1851-1853), to Morris himself (*The Defence of Guenevere*, 1858).

The earlier origins of epic fantasy, of course, are in a direct line from the fabulous epics of Gilgamesh, Ulysses, Finn Mac Coul, Siegfried, Beowulf, Arthur, Charlemagne and, again primarily through Morris, the Icelandic sagas.

If I fail to define epic fantasy (except very roughly and in passing) in this essay I shall also fail to defend it for its own sake. As with anything else, only a little is outstandingly good and much of it, while it has attractive qualities of enthusiasm and vitality, has no literary merit. I'm unable to muster much nostalgic response to most old sf magazines, comic books or that school of fiction exemplified by Oxford's deceased Inklings. I admire intelligent, disciplined, imaginative entertainment if it seems to offer me some perspective on my own life. This essay, therefore, cannot be the celebration of a form. It can only praise individuals. Similarly I will not be mentioning my own work or that which has most obviously derived from it. As it is, I shall only be able to deal briefly with many of the writers discussed, and I'm aware that I frequently fail to support my cases as fully as I should. If this is particularly irritating to you, I apologize. When I wrote the bulk of this essay I was first and foremost a polemecist arguing for improved standards in popular fiction. In many cases those standards have improved considerably and there are now many good writers providing us with substantial examples. That many of these have turned to what used to be called science fantasy for their inspiration could support my argument about the poor standards of most Tolkien-influenced heroic fantasy. Sadly, they can't be the subject of this essay, but I have added a few recent pieces as a sort of appendix to this, to point the reader in the direction of the kind of work I favour. Lastly, most of the sweeping statements found here may be regarded as the opening stages of a debate rather than final pronouncements of my own faith. I am primarily arguing against what was received opinion at the time I wrote the earliest version of this introduction in the early 1960s and therefore beg your indulgence.

H. P. Lovecraft, always in my view a somewhat inadequate describer of the indescribable, says in his book *Marginalia*:

Modern Science has, in the end, proved an enemy to art and pleasure; for by revealing to us the whole sordid and prosaic basis of our thoughts, motives and acts, it has stripped the world of glamour, wonder, and all those illusions of heroism, nobility, and sacrifice which used to sound so impressive when romantically treated. Indeed, it is not too much to say that psychological discovery, and chemical, physical and psychological research have largely destroyed the element of emotion among informed and sophisticated people by resolving it into its component parts.

There is pathos in this statement, as well as a rather unappealing kind of aggression expressed by many disappointed conservative critics of modern life and for me it helps explain why I can never enjoy a Lovecraft story. His words are all but meaningless. The heroism, nobility and sacrifice of Rudolf Hess may be moving, but they are only "impressive" if we understand the psychology involved. I believe that critical dissection of the fantasy story into its components does not detract from the story. Rather it adds a new dimension to it; a dimension which to me is far more interesting and rewarding. In an article published in the *Woman Journalist* (Spring 1963) J. G. Ballard wrote

I feel that the writer of fantasy has a marked tendency to select images and ideas which directly reflect the internal landscapes of his mind, and the reader of fantasy must interpret them on this level distinguishing between the manifest content, which may seem obscure, meaningless or nightmarish, and the latent content, the private vocabulary of symbols drawn by the narrative from the writer's mind. The dream worlds, synthetic landscapes and plasticity of visual forms invented by the writer of fantasy are external equivalents of the inner world of the psyche....

In modern times Einstein, Freud and Jung among them have

broadened rather than destroyed the scope of the artist and broadened the range of meaning and pleasure which the intelligent reader can derive from fiction. In a romance the "real" world of the social novel is reversed; the protagonists are placed in landscapes directly reflecting the inner landscapes of their minds. A hero might range the terrain of his own psyche, encountering, as other characters, various aspects of himself. It's perfectly possible, therefore, that a good fantasy story could to lead us to greater self-understanding.

For me the main fascination of the fantasy story lies in its manipulation of direct subconscious symbols. The mingled attraction and revulsion often felt by its readers might well express the combined curiosity and fear of seeing too deeply into themselves. If our "irrational" dreams are potent images "explained" by the semi-conscious mind and blended into some sort of rough plot, so fantasy stories take the same material and attempt the same sort of job, with the object of convincing our rational minds, even if only temporarily. Too much rationalization, and we get a certain kind of rather dull science fiction; just enough to organize the images and give symbolic shape to and perhaps understanding of our strongest, most secret impulses, and we get a good fantasy story. Add superior language and we get a Coleridge or a Tennyson. Add irony and we get a degree of objectivity reflected, say, in the work of Borges or Calvino.

Epic fantasy can offer a world of metaphor in which to explore the rich, hidden territories deep within us. And this, of course, is why epic romances, romantic poetry, grotesques, fascinated painters and illustrators for centuries, just as fabulous and mythological subjects have always inspired them, as representations of this inner world. The romance's prime concern is not with character or narrative but with the evocation of strong, powerful images; symbols conjuring up a multitude of sensations to be used (as mystics once used distorting mirrors, as romantics used opium or, latterly, LSD) as escape from the pressures of the objective world or as a means of achieving increased self-awareness.

In some cases the writer and the illustrator have been combined in one person (Blake, Rossetti, Wyndham Lewis, Peake). Even if we exclude all the children's writers (Ruskin/Doyle, Carroll/Tenniel, Nesbit/Millar, Baum/Neill) who have had long associations with particular illustrators, there are a good few adult writers of fantasy who have enjoyed similar relationships—Dunsany and Sime, Cabell and Papé, Burroughs and St. John, Howard and Frazetta. There are innumerable versions of Goethe, Poe, the Arabian Nights, Hans Andersen, Hoffman, Wagner, from the "Golden Age" of illustration. More recently, artists have been attracted to the work of epic fantasts like Tolkien, Hodgson, Howard, Leiber as inspiration for elaborate posters, lavishly illustrated books and comic strip adaptations. Many of the best artists are attracted to these works because they tend to emphasize human aspiration and foibles, their pathos and ecstasy, more directly than, say, science fiction (itself, really, only a branch of fabulous romantic fiction). Since the 1960s there has been a huge revival of the art of book illustration, primarily based around this kind of fiction. From somewhat crude beginnings, where artists (as the bad ones still do) hid poor draughtsmanship behind elaborate grotesqueries, there is now developing a variety of excellent illustrators.

If, currently, the morbidly sexual aspects of fantasy are in danger of becoming a stale convention by virtue of repetition, if distorted perspective and two-dimensional sensationalism, inherited from the conventions of the commercial comic strip, still tend to dominate the magazines, comics and posters, equally there are signs of artists maturing both technically and emotionally. We see their work becoming increasingly subtle and humane; their ambitions growing as their mastery of their art grows and their talents—inspired by an increasing number of peers, by an increasing public appreciation of good work, by the appearance, in recent years, of publishers who both respect the artists and are prepared to pay them fair rates— blooming as luxuriantly throughout Europe and America as they did in that "golden age" of Willette, Beardsley, Klimt, Mucha, Dulac, Bull, Sime, Pogany, the Robinsons and all the other fabulous illustrators who emerged between the 1880s and the beginning of the First World War.

Lastly, it could be argued that the present time is in many ways the worst in which to try to assess current developments in fantastic fiction. We are currently experiencing a boom in this, the youngest and generally most successful of publishing/bookselling categories. Whereas writers of epic fantasy might, like me, get irritated a few years ago because bookshops insisted on putting all their work in the sf section, now those same writers inhabit a section marked simply Fantasy and have covers on their books which are almost invariably indistinguishable from a hundred others. Therefore it's pretty hard to see the wood for the trees. In order to write this essay I originally read a fair number of recent books in this category but cannot claim to have read all the best or all the worst. Most of them are simply bad, several show promise, one or two are by writers of genuinely original talent. If names are omitted by me it is not especially significant. I've no wish to attack the work of new and young writers, many of whom will doubtless find their feet in genre work before producing something more individual. In the main I have saved my polemics for writers who already have large (and often highly inflated) reputations. I have also preferred to quote those writers I admire, rather than take to task those I dislike. I hope that my relish for the work of the writers I enjoy will be what the reader remembers best from this essay which functions increasingly, I suspect, as a work of historical interest, discussing the origins of a genre which now dominates the best-seller charts and supplies the content of many hugely successful films.

I would like to thank various people for their help on this book. Firstly, as always, my wife Linda Steele, who read the text and helped produce the final edited version. Parts of this essay appeared in different forms in *Science Fantasy* magazine, 1963-64 (commissioned by E. J. Carnell), in *Foundation* (editor Malcolm Edwards) and elsewhere, or have been given as talks to the Second World Fantasy Convention (who kindly invited me as Guest of Honor, New York, 1976), the Oxford Literary Society, the Cambridge Literary Society, Eton College Literary Society and others, to whom I am very grateful. "Epic Pooh" was published in pamphlet form by the British Fantasy Society, 1976. Parts have also appeared in the *London Daily News*, *Exploring Fantasy Worlds*, Borgo Press, 1985 and *Fantasists on Fantasy*, Avon Books, 1984. The original text was written at the request of Philip Dunn of the now defunct Pierrot Publishing. The revised text was commissioned by David Hartwell (then chief editor of Timescape Books, who left before I could deliver it!). Thanks also to John Clute, for reading the manuscript and giving me his useful comments. A version of "Origins" was originally written in 1964 for Langdon Jones's magazine *Tensor*, but never published.

I'm grateful to Mr. Jones for supplying me with the only existing copy. People have been helpful in making suggestions for reading and so on. Among these are David Tate, Colin Greenland, Terri Windling, Brian Tawn, Roz Kaveney, Chelsea Quinn Yarbro, Lisa Tuttle and last but not least Messrs. Dave Gibson and Ted Ball (of Fantasy Centre bookshop) and John Eggeling (of Phantasmagoria Books) who supplied many of the titles.

Lastly I would like to add that the appendices were included without the knowledge of Messrs. Miéville and VanderMeer, but before I had seen their generous introduction and afterword!

Michael Moorcock
Ingleton, W. Yorks,
August 1977
Fulham Road, London,
December 1985
Point Reyes Station, California,
August 2003

I
ORIGINS

Such a doze as I then enjoyed, I find compatible with indulging the best and deepest cogitations which at any time arise in my mind. I chew the cud of sweet and bitter fancy, in a state betwixt sleeping and waking, which I consider so highly favourable to philosophy, that I have no doubt some of its most distinguished systems have been composed under its influence. My servant is, therefore, instructed to tread as if upon down—my door-hinges are carefully oiled—and all appliances used to prevent me from being prematurely and harshly called back to the broad waking-day of a laborious world. My custom, in this particular, is so well known, that the very school-boys cross the alley on tip-toe, betwixt the hours of four and five. My cell is the very dwelling of Morpheus. There is indeed a bawling knave of a broom-man, *quem ego*—but this is a matter for the Quarter-Sessions.

Sir Walter Scott, Introduction to *Peveril of the Peak*

Perhaps the main fascination of epic fantasy is that there have been few basic changes in it for centuries. I am referring specifically to that body of prose fiction distinguished from myth, legend and folk-tale by its definite authorship and not genuinely purporting to be a true account of historical or religious events. Therefore the *Nibelungenlied, La Chanson de Roland, Le Morte d'Arthur* by Malory, or *Le Cid* by Corneille are not fantasy fiction.

For the purposes of discussion the *Arabian Nights* or Moncrief's *Adventures de Zeloide et d'Amanzarifdine* and many other groups of Oriental stories must also be set aside together with the large body of tales of Arab chivalry especially popular during the centuries of Moslem domination of the Spanish peninsula.

The body of literature incorporating marvels and fantasies is so vast that it would be impossible in a short book to discuss it all. Fantastic fiction, as opposed to the folk epic, is like the majority of modern fiction primarily fashionable, written for a particular audience at a particular time. Although it borrows images and cadences from poetry it is almost never poetic. It caters for current tastes; it takes the elements from the mother-body and presents them in popular and sensational form, working them into shapes and styles owing much to the demands of its contemporary audiences. Though occasionally it will transcend these limitations it rarely outlives its audience. Popular fantasy fiction is not to be confused with the work of Spenser, Milton, Goethe, the major Romantics, *Ossian* and the Celtic Romance, satirists like Anatole France in, say, *La Revolte des anges*, allegorists such as Bunyan and Wyndham Lewis (or, during the later part of his career, John Cowper Powys), Hesse, Calvino or Borges. Epic fantasy includes *The Lord of the Rings*, *Conan the Conqueror* and *Palmerin of England*.

Palmerin de Ingelaterra (1547-48) and thousands like it were to the public of the 16th century what *Star Wars*, *Indiana Jones, The Matrix,* and horror movies are to the public of the 21st. They are called "decadent" or "artificial" Romances and today most of them are, like most of the Gothic novels and oriental tales of the late 18th and early 19th centuries, virtually unreadable. *Palmerin* was, with *Amadis of Gaul*, one of the chivalric romances which escaped burning by the barber and the curate in *Don Quixote*, Cervantes' satire on such books. It was regarded, therefore, as a cut above the rest. Nonetheless these romances were fantasies in that their chief purpose was to amaze and shock. They are packed with wizards, magic weapons, cloaks of invisibility, beautiful sorceresses, flying machines and diving bells of various unlikely kinds, magic cups, rings, crowns, shoes, horses and castles; ogres, dwarves, monsters, malevolent spirits, helpful spirits, black curses, doom, tragedy, the folk of Faery and a hero of incredible youth, good looks and prowess who is out to rescue a heroine of incredible youth, beauty and virtue.

> Before heaven, your worship should read what I have read, concerning Felixmarte of Hyrcania, who with one backstroke cut asunder five giants through the middle, as if they had been so many bean-cods.... At another time he encountered a great and powerful army, consisting of about a million six hundred thousand soldiers, all armed from head to foot, and routed them as if they had been a flock of sheep. But what will you say of the good Don Cirongilo of Thrace? who was so stout and valiant...that once as he was sailing on a river, seeing a fiery serpent rise to the surface of the water, he immediately threw himself upon it, and getting astride its scaly shoulders squeezed its throat with both hands with so much force that the serpent, finding itself in danger of being choked, had no other remedy but to plunge to the bottom of the river, carrying with him the knight, who would not quit his hold; and when they reached the bottom, he found himself in such a fine palace and beautiful gardens, that it was wonderful; and presently the serpent turned into an old man, who said so many things to him that the like was never heard.
>
> *Don Quixote*

Deriving from the Romances of Arthur, Charlemagne and the Cid, owing something to Greek and Roman epics, something to fable and a little to history, borrowing language and manners from the metrical epics, from Ariosto, from *Aucassin et Nicolette*, the decadent Chivalric Romances had superficial resemblances to the originals but lacked their beauty of language and their genuine tragic elements. It is the mark of commercial writers that they cheerfully disguise or dispense with the tragic implications of their material, sentimentalize relationships, intentions, even landscape, if it wins the approval of their audience.

The Gothic Romance, which grew to popularity during the Romantic Revival, had much of its origins in the Chivalric Romance, but emphasized the element of terror and attempted, usually, to rationalize the supernatural element. It replaced chivalric notions with the ideals of its predominantly bourgeois audience. It made use of techniques developed by Defoe, Grimmelshausen, Richardson or Fielding and no longer bore any resemblance to folk-literature.

However, in its use of archetypal characters, scenery and plots, the Gothic was still connected very closely to the Chivalric Romance, just as the modern tale of lost lands, prehistoric civilizations, fairy kingdoms or distant planets is connected to them both.

A student of five hundred years hence will be unlikely to see much difference between all of these. As the Gothic lost popularity and passed its lasting qualities into the general mainstream of fiction so, for instance, will the science fiction romance leave its mark only on juvenile adventure stories and on the range of technique and reference available to the writer of non-category fiction.

Conscious art is on the whole lacking from the decadent Romance. Ornate and elaborate euphemism is substituted for the direct, simple language of the metrical romance or the poetry of *Orlando Furioso*. The sense of high tragedy found in the story of Tristram and Isolde is never apparent. In place of these are marvels upon marvels. The magical and supernatural elements in the great epics rarely dominated the human conflict. They served symbolically, to heighten it. To modern readers of these epics the weighty narrative machinery, the dialogues and diversions, the archaisms are forgotten as the story gathers force, finding constant echoes in the reader's own experience, resonances in their remembered dreams. Though concerned with deeds of daring, magic, and human love there are no such resonances in the decadent Romance and so a modern reader's interest soon flags. To keep them reading such a book must be written in more or less idiomatic language, in a certain kind of undemanding, colloquial tone, for it is offering nothing but sensation and escapism.

Instead of

> He gave him a good sword in his hand,
> His head therewith for to keep;
> And there where the wall was lowest,

Anon down did they leap.

By that the cock began to crow,
The day began to spring;
The sheriff found the jailor dead,
The common bell made he ring.

He made a cry throughout the town,
Whether he be yeoman or knave,
That could bring him Robin Hood,
His warison he should have.
A Tale of Robin Hood, c. 1350

we get

When he was seven years old, King Languines and
his queen and household, passing through his
kingdom from one town to another, came to the castle
of Gandales, where they were feasted; but the Child
of the Sea, and Gandalin, and the other children were
removed to the back court, that they might not be
seen....
Southey's 1807 translation *Amadis of Gaul,*
Montalvo, 1508

Then Palmerin and Trineus, snatching their lances
from their dwarves, and clasping their helmets,
galloped amain after the giant, and Palmerin, having
gotten a sight of him, came posting amain, saying:
"Stay, traitorous thief, for thou mayst not so carry
away her, that is worth the greatest lord in the world!"
and with these words, gave him a blow on the
shoulder, that he struck him besides his elephant. ...
Palmerin de Oliva, c. 1511, quoted in Beaumont's
Knight of the Burning Pestle, c. 1610

Palmerin of England was very popular in Tudor England and
has a sequel, *Palmerin de Oliva.* Allegedly written by a king of

Portugal and sometimes thought to be the work of an unknown woman, it was probably by Francisco de Moroes. *Amadis of Gaul* was also Portuguese in origin. This was the most imitated. The original four printed volumes were followed by about fifty sequels from almost as many imitators.

Amadis is included in the body of Romance usually termed Peninsula since it originated in Christian Spain, Portugal and Italy. It is marked by a heavy Oriental influence and it was probably the same influence (stemming from such works as the *Arabian Nights*) which gave it its highly fantastic flavour.

These first four volumes of *Amadis* retain much of the drama of their earlier counterparts. This is primarily because they hinge on a classical plot and retain the range of archetypes. Because the average reader is not likely to have a copy to hand I intend to give here the only plot summary to be found in this book.

Amadis is born of an illegitimate union between Elisena, daughter of the King of Brittany, and King Perion of "Gaul" (probably Wales). Because of the stigma he is placed in a coracle and thrown into a river which runs to the sea. The coracle is found by Sir Gandales of Scotland who rears the boy with Gandalin, his son. He is nicknamed "the Child of the Sea," and he and Gandalin become inseparable. Sir Gandales knows that his foster child is the son of a king, since there is a note to that effect in the coracle, as well as an assortment of tokens to prove it.

Progressing through his kingdom from one town to another, King Languines of Scotland and his wife stay at the castle of Sir Gandales where they take a fancy to "the Child of the Sea" and his foster brother, bringing them to court as companions for their son Agraies. Little do any of them know that Languines's queen is actually Amadis's aunt. Soon we hear that Perion and Elisena have married. Amadis is legitimate! The couple have another son, Galaor, who is kidnapped by a giant, one Gandalac, who plans to bring the boy up to avenge a wrong done him. A simple-minded soul, Gandalac gives Galaor into the keeping of a hermit who moulds him into a heroic and chivalrous youth. Perion and Elisena have a third son, Florestan, who serves no narrative purpose save to make the story more confusing. Giants and evil knights are fought by Amadis, Galaor and Florestan, with Gandalin tagging along as squire, but the brothers are still unaware of their relationship.

Then Perion decides to visit Languines's Court at the same time as Lisuarte, King of Great Britain, who has brought Oriana, his daughter, with him. Oriana will become the story's heroine. After many, many pages of confused activity, Amadis accomplishes a quantity of doughty deeds and then his parentage is discovered. There is a full-scale reunion somewhat reminiscent of *The Man Who Was Thursday* or one of those skits on comic-strip super-heroes who reveal their secret identities all at once. The love of Amadis for Oriana is declared and we're off on a new set of adventures which are of a simpler construction and easier to follow. They are extraordinarily reminiscent of an Edgar Rice Burroughs yarn. The mistaken identity theme is familiar in all fiction and is often used to maintain certain conventional tensions in narratives which would otherwise fall to pieces after chapter three.

The set of stories is quite sharply divided between the initial tangle ending with recognitions and joyful discovery, a long episode involving a misunderstanding between the lovers (shades of P. G. Wodehouse as well as Edgar Rice Burroughs) and a kidnapping sequence where Oriana is taken to the enchanted Firm Island and Amadis has to rescue her. The fourth volume ends on this note.

Also in the two latter sequences we are introduced to Urganda the Unknown, a beneficent sorceress, mysterious and wise, and Arcalaus, who has been described as "an enchanter-at-arms" and "one of the largest knights in the world who were not giants." Amadis and Galaor are the two central characters here and they are contrasted quite well—Amadis remaining true to Oriana throughout, whereas Galaor is always indulging in diversions of love. The most concentrated fantastic element is in the Firm Island sequences.

The Firm Island had been the home of Apollidon, "the sagest of enchanters," who had lived there with his wife Grimanesa. He had built a huge, jewel-studded castle and gardens and orchards that bloomed and bore fruit throughout the year. "Never had been such magnificence, nor such marvels as the lord of this land gathered together by his wealth and by his magic arts." However, though he had hoped to spend his old age on the Firm Island, Apollidon was asked to go to Greece and there be crowned Emperor: "Then he left the Firm Island, with all its wonders, as a heritage to any knight who should prove as brave in arms as himself and as loyal in love to a lady not less fair and faithful than his own wife. To test the virtues of all aspirants, he laid mystic spells on the island, only to be broken by him who should be its lord. At the entrance to the gardens was an arch that could be safely passed by none but true lovers; and in the midst of them stood a Forbidden Chamber, fast closed to all but the knight and lady destined to achieve such great adventure. A hundred years had passed since the spell was laid, and a hundred knights had vainly sought to break it, when Amadis came with his kinsman to visit the Firm Island."

Amadis, Agraies, Galaor and Florestan come to the Arch of True Lovers which is guarded by a huge copper giant with a trumpet at its mouth. If an untrue lover tries to enter, the trumpet will blast him down with smoke and flames, but if he is true, music will issue from the trumpet. Agraies dashes through the gate and the trumpet blows sweet music and exquisite perfume.

"On the other side he came to statues of Apollidon and Grimanesa so artfully fashioned that he thought they smiled on him, and at their feet a table of jasper on which were carved the names of those knights who had come through aforetime. Now, while he read he saw with amazement his own name springing to view..."

Amadis also enters and sees his name appear, but his brothers demur—they are pretty sure they won't get sweet music and perfume....

As Amadis and Agraies stroll about the beautiful gardens, Amadis's dwarf servant Ardian tells them that his brothers have got themselves into a mess. They have asked where the Forbidden Chamber lies and are debating whether to pass by the two pillars, one brass, one marble, which are on its path.

Florestan reaches the brazen pillar.

"But ere he had reached it was soon to be fighting as if with the air. From all sides hailed upon him heavy blows dealt by invisible enemies, and when he struck back he felt his sword's edge turned upon ghostly weapons besetting him at every step."

Florestan is hurled back at his brother's feet to lie as though dead. At this Galaor plunges in, makes out a little better, but is finally also hurled back. They are soon revived, however, as the cousins turn up. Agraies tries his luck and is unsuccessful. "None can fight through this enchantment but the peer of Apollidon who devised it," says the Governor of the Island. Amadis, of course, wins through to the Forbidden Chamber and the enchantment is broken.

This episode serves to prove to Oriana that Amadis is a true lover after all. But the story isn't over. Further complications arise and Amadis disguises himself as Beltenbros, since he doesn't know that Oriana no longer hates him and has been living in a hermitage mourned as dead by his friends. As "Beltenbros" he comes home to find a war brewing between the King of Ireland (whose son he killed earlier) and King Lisuarte. Disguised in black and silver armour he joins the ranks of Lisuarte and there follows a battle scene between Cildadan of Ireland and Lisuarte of Great Britain which is reminiscent of the battles for which Robert E. Howard is famous. Here is a further quote from Moncrieff's excellent precis in *Romance and Legend of Chivalry* (Gresham, c. 1912):

> Lisuarte welcomed Beltenbros, whose aid he could not refuse, since he now got news how was lost to him one of his trustiest warriors, Arban of Wales. He had been made prisoner by the wife of Famongomadan in revenge for her husband's death, and was pining in that giant's dungeons till the king were able to deliver him. Beltenbros made up the tale of his party, all of them famous knights of their time. There were the brothers of Amadis, and his cousin Agraies of Scotland; and Gandalac, Galaor's foster-father, with his sons Gavus and Palomir, Bramadil; and Nicoran, Keeper of the Perilous Bridge, with Dragonis and Palomar, and Pinorante; Gimontes, the king's nephew; the renowned Sir Bruneo of Bonamar, who, before Amadis had achieved the passage of the True Lover's Arch, also his brother Branfil; and Sir Guilan the Pensive; and good old Sir Grumedan, who bore the king's banner in the centre of the troop, and Ladasin, and Galvanes, and Olivas; and many another whose name should not be forgotten.
>
> On the adverse side, also, were chiefs of renown,

and some of gigantic stature, such as Cartadaque, Albadanzor, and Gadancuriel, whom King Cildadan placed in the front of his ranks. He missed that day Famongomadan and his mighty son Basagente, who had been laid low by Beltenbros on their way to take part in the battle. But not less fearful was the giant Mandanfabul, lord of the Isle of the Vermillion Tower, who with ten of his like were placed in the rear on a hill, with orders not to engage till they saw the enemy broken and weary, then to rush down upon King Lisuarte and kill him or carry him off prisoner.

The trumpet gave the signal for both lines to close, breaking upon each other like waves foaming with steel. The ground shook under the crash of that onset, in which many a man went down, and many a horse galloped away without a rider. Soon all the field was hidden in clouds of dust, where the fighters, panting for heat and rage, were mixed in a confused struggle; and those who looked on with throbbing hearts could not tell how it went with friend or foe. But like a thunderbolt gleamed through the medley that silver knight on a black horse, that kept ever close to the old king, when, caring not to live unless victorious, he threw himself into the hottest press.

The battle lasts half a day and all are weary until "through the thinned ranks swooped Mandanfabul with his band of fresh fighters, like kites upon their prey, and came charging towards the royal banner." They carry Lisuarte off, but Beltenbros/Amadis sees Mandanfabul riding away with the king and gives chase. "…He soon came up with Mandanfabul, and fetched him such a mighty blow as not only shore off the giant's right arm, but beneath it cut through Lisuarte's armour and drew his blood. Mandanfabul losing control of his horse, was carried away bleeding to death." Amadis returns to rally the flagging knights. "Then over all the clang and clamour rang out his warcry:

'Gaul! Gaul! I am Amadis!'"

And, given fresh courage by the sight of the famed hero, the knights of Amadis beat the knights of the King of Ireland.

In this episode we are given a mystic prophecy from Urganda the Unknown, together with various monsters and giants and magics of all kinds. It is scarcely different in any way (save for the element of chivalry) from, say, Howard's *Conan the Conqueror*, whose plot is written in a livelier style, is slightly less rambling and is considerably shorter.

As an example of one of the best artificial Romances, *Amadis* probably deserves its preservation. Its imitators, though containing many more marvels (a large number directly derived from Arabian tales), are interesting only for their variety of enchantments and spells. *Palmerin of England* is one of the few real rivals, though it is quite similar in most ways to *Amadis*.

The Chivalric Romance, together with old English metrical ballads (as published in Percy's *Reliques*) and Macpherson's *Ossian* forgeries, influenced two important and connected strains in English literature: the historical novel of Scott and others, and the Gothic "tale of terror" which in its earliest form usually had a mediaeval setting.

Many writers have discussed the reasons for their appeal. Robert Graves's *The White Goddess* provides a semi-mystical explanation; Jung's *Modern Man in Search of a Soul* provides a psychological one. The best single work on purely literary aspects is probably Mario Praz's *The Romantic Agony*.

The first Gothic romance to call itself that and to begin the vogue for tales of terror was Walpole's *Castle of Otranto* (1764). Walpole's main interest was art and architecture. By "Gothic" he meant pre-Renaissance. Just as *Don Quixote* and *The Knight of the Burning Pestle* had appeared as a reaction against the Romance, Walpole's book was a reaction against the prevailing classicism of the Age of Reason, directly opposed in its intentions to the pseudo-realism of Defoe, Richardson or Fielding. With Macpherson's *Fingal* (1762) and Percy's *Reliques of Ancient English Poetry* (1765) it is generally thought to be one of the chief landmarks of the beginning of the Romantic Revival. Clara Reeve's *The Champion of Virtue, a Gothic Story* (1777) was written in deliberate homage to Walpole. Set in the 15th century it contains a great deal of description of romantic landscape and architecture but only one supernatural element (a ghost). It was later reissued as *The Old English Baron* and, like Walpole's romance, remains in print.

Although neither book is, in itself, especially appealing to modern taste, they are important because they represent a watershed in the development of fiction. They did not merely look back to "romantic, antique days"; they borrowed many techniques from Defoe (with his verisimilitude, his realistic attention to detail) and Richardson (his sentiment) and they added something novel in the emphasis given to natural (if often idealized) scenery as a means of expressing the moods of the characters. Like the Brontës, they took the internal landscapes of the mind and gave them external form.

> The Gothic castle itself, that formidable place, ruinous yet an effective prison, phantasmagorically shifting its outline as ever new vaults extended from their labyrinths, scene of solitary wanderings, cut off from light and human contact, of unformulated menace and the terror of the living dead—this hold, with all its hundred names, now looms to investigators as the symbol of a neurosis; they see it as the gigantic symbol of anxiety, the dread of oppression and of the abyss, the response to the...insecurity of disturbed times.
>
> Herbert Read, Introduction, *The Gothic Flame*

The popularity of the Gothic rose as the impact of the Industrial Revolution increased, reflecting, symbolizing and even explaining the anxiety felt by those who witnessed radical changes in the world they knew. There are parallels today between the popularity of science fiction and powerful social changes with which we are all familiar. Invasions from outer space are symbolic versions of a threat to one's habitual way of life. Those flying saucers and cigars carry cargoes of the terrors we rarely admit to and refuse to examine. The historical romance is still there to satisfy those who look back to a simpler past, but it lacks the substance of its Gothic ancestors.

> The savageness of Gothic stands for wildness of thought and roughness of work, and impresses upon us the image of a race full of wolfish life, and an

imagination as wild and wayward as the northern seas. The darkened air, the pile of buttresses and rugged walls uncouthly hewn out of rocks over wild moors, speak of the savageness of their massy architecture, which was rude, ponderous, stiff, sombre and depressing.

Devendra P. Varma, *The Gothic Flame*

Admirers of Howard and Lovecraft will probably recognize the appeal of the Gothic.

The best of the Gothic novelists are Walpole, Ann Radcliffe, William Beckford, William Godwin, Matthew Gregory Lewis, Mary Shelley and Charles Maturin. Unlike the Chivalric Romances, their work is easily obtainable.

Mrs. Radcliffe's books, like most other Gothics, involved a wicked nobleman dwelling in a massive and oppressive Gothic castle, part of which was ruined. The wicked nobleman pursues and incarcerates, incarcerates and pursues the pure heroine through the labyrinthine corridors of his castle until she is finally rescued by the upright hero who is likely to be the true heir to the castle and its lands. This basic plot was, with a few exceptions, virtually the only plot of the Gothics, and the mixture was varied by its choice of supernatural events, although several spectres were always included. Ann Radcliffe is considered its greatest exponent. Here she describes her heroine's first sight of Udolpho:

> Emily gazed with melancholy awe upon the castle…for, though it was now lighted up by the setting sun, the Gothic greatness of its features, and its mouldering walls of dark grey stone, rendered it a gloomy and sublime object….The light died away on its walls, leaving a melancholy purple tint, which spread deeper and deeper as the thin vapour crept up the mountain, while the battlements above were still tipped with splendour….Silent, lonely, and sublime, it seemed to stand the sovereign of the scene and to frown defiance on all who dared its solitary reign. As the twilight deepened, its features became more aweful in obscurity…till its clustering towers

were alone seen rising above the tops of the woods....
The extent and darkness of these tall woods
awakened terrific images in her mind....[She] soon
after reached the castle gates, where the deep tone
of the portal bell...increased the fearful emotions that
had assailed [her]....She anxiously surveyed the
edifice; but the gloom that overspread it allowed her
to distinguish little more than...the massy walls of
the ramparts, and to know that it was vast, ancient
and dreary.
The Mysteries of Udolpho

This was the sort of thing which was to influence Byron, Shelley, Wordsworth, Coleridge and de Quincey. It was to influence Mary Shelley, Edgar Allan Poe, Bram Stoker and all those writers whose work, via the motion picture screen, has given the world new myths and folk-tales. It influenced Scott, of course, and resulted in the foundation of a lasting form of historical romance. Directly or indirectly it influenced Lovecraft and the *Weird Tales* writers:

...A certain huge, dark church...stood out with
especial distinctness at certain hours of the day, and
at sunset the great tower and tapering steeple loomed
blackly against the flaming sky. It seemed to rest on
especially high ground; for the grimy facade, and the
obliquely seen north side with sloping roof and the
tops of great pointed windows, rose boldly above
the tangle of surrounding ridgepoles and chimney-
pots. Peculiarly grimy and austere, it appeared to be
built of stone, stained and weathered with the smoke
and storms of a century or more. The style, so far as
the glass could show, was the earliest experimental
form of Gothic revival....The longer he watched the
more his imagination worked, till at length he began
to fancy curious things.
Lovecraft, "The Haunter of the Dark"

Goethe, Fenimore Cooper, Dumas, Hugo, Balzac, Sue, and all the French Romantics were to be influenced by the Gothic in one way or another. Crude in themselves these tales spawned an enormous variety of work and in popular form their style and content has hardly changed at all. As Dr. Varma says in *The Gothic Flame*, "The Gothic novels present no restful human shades of grey: the characters are mostly either endowed with sombre, diabolical villainy or pure angelic virtue. Interfering fathers, brutal in threats, oppress the hero or heroine into a loathed marriage; officials of the Inquisition or the characters of abbots and abbesses are imbued with fiendish cruelty, often gloating in Gothic diabolism over their tortures."

Evil monks and nuns were often central characters in the Gothics—the cowl shading the face was of particular appeal. Ruined castles, abbeys, convents, labyrinths, hidden vaults, overpowering natural scenery are standard to almost all of them. Supplying the fantastic element, perhaps unconsciously as a respectable substitute for de Sade's more outrageous developments, we find vampires, werewolves, ghosts of assorted kinds, portraits that come suddenly to life, witches' sabbats, walking corpses and, indeed, all the familiar supernatural elements beloved of Hammer films and Roger Corman. The sexual aspects, of course, are always disguised and only in Lewis's *The Monk* do they ever threaten to reveal themselves for what they are. A terror of normal sexuality is another common theme (see the quote below from John Norman, page 94). The character of Lewis's monk, Ambrosio, who changes from a blameless and pure life to one of rape, torture, murder, necromancy and incest, is unforgettable. It is, as it were, a Freudian's dream, with its emphasis on violence, slimy filth, loathsome creatures, drenching blood. "Often," says the incarcerated nun Agnes, "have I sat waking found my fingers ringed with the long worms which bred in the corrupted flesh of my infant." As in many such books there is a version of the Faustian theme beloved of conservative writers of Romance. Ambrosio has sold his soul to the devil, but pays a dreadful penalty:

> Ambrosio started, and expected the demon with terror....The thunder ceasing to roll a full strain of melodious music sounded in the air! At the same time the cloud disappeared, and he beheld a figure more beautiful than fancy's pencil ever drew. It was a youth seemingly scarce eighteen, the perfection of whose form and face was unrivalled. He was perfectly naked,

a bright star sparkled on his forehead, two crimson
wings extended themselves from his shoulders, and
his silken locks were confined by a band of many-
coloured fires, which shone with a brilliancy far
surpassing that of precious stones. Circlets of
diamonds were fastened around his arms and ankles,
and in his right hand he bore a silver branch imitating
myrtle. His form shone with dazzling glory: he was
surrounded by clouds of rose-coloured light, and at
the moment that he appeared a refreshing air breathed
perfumes throughout the cavern. Ambrosio gazed
upon the spirit with delight and wonder.
The Monk

As, until recently, in generic science fiction and fantasy, there is
very little overt eroticism in most Gothic novels and many habitual
readers of Gothics, content to enjoy the hidden and somewhat morbid
joys of the form, reacted against *The Monk* when it first appeared in
1796.

Maturin's *Melmoth the Wanderer*, the tale of a doomed near-
immortal who lives for 150 years enjoying (or being told about)
many strange adventures, is probably the longest and most ambitious
of these stories and one of my favourites. Here, too, is morbid
sexuality, supernatural horror and the rest, but it is crystallized and
utilized to more significant effect. The narrative technique is
complicated and likely to annoy the modern reader (it consists of a
series of tales, each inside the other) but the character of Melmoth is
perfectly described. To me he is a better character than (and the
ancestor of) Roderic Usher. Possibly also he is an ancestor of Dorian
Gray and Mr. Hyde. The early part of this four-volume novel describes
how an Englishman named Stanton pursues Melmoth, obsessed by
the mystery surrounding him. He meets him, on one occasion, after
visiting the theatre.

When the play was over, he stood for some moments
in the deserted streets. It was a beautiful moonlight
night, and he saw near him a figure, whose shadow,
projected half across the street, (there were no flagged

ways then, chains and posts were the only defence of the foot passenger), appeared to him of gigantic magnitude. He had been so long accustomed to contend with these phantoms of the imagination, that he took a kind of stubborn delight in subduing them. He walked up to the object, and observing the shadow only was magnified, and the figure was the ordinary height of a man, he approached it, and discovered the very object of his search—the man whom he had seen for a moment in Valentia, and, after a search of four years, recognized at the theatre.

"You were in quest of me?" —"I was." "Have you any thing to inquire of me?" —"Much." "Speak, then." —"This is no place." "No place! poor wretch, I am independent of time and place. Speak, if you have any thing to ask or to learn?" —"I have many things to ask, but nothing to learn, I hope, from you." "You deceive yourself, but you will be undeceived when next we meet." —"And when shall that be~" said Stanton, grasping his arm; "name your hour and your place." "The hour shall be mid-day," answered the stranger, with a horrid and unintelligible smile; "and the place shall be the bare walls of a madhouse, where you shall rise rattling in your chains, and rustling from your straw, to greet me—yet still you shall have *the curse of sanity*, and of memory. My voice shall ring in your ears till then, and the glance of these eyes shall be reflected from every object, animate or inanimate, till you behold them again." —"Is it under circumstances so horrible we are to meet again?" said Stanton, shrinking under the full-lighted blaze of those demon eyes. "I never," said the stranger, in an emphatic tone —"I *never desert my friends in misfortune*. When they are plunged in the lowest abyss of human calamity, *they are sure to be visited by me*."
Melmoth the Wanderer

Melmoth is the devil's agent, given immortality as long as he can supply new victims to his master. He visits those in distress (as Stanton is in distress according to his prophecy) offering them aid in return for their souls. But this we aren't told for hundreds of pages and it is a tribute to Maturin that he holds our attention through dozens of digressions. In Godwin, in Beckford, in Mary Shelley and Maturin, in Mrs. Dacre's *Zofloya, the Diabolical Moor*, science is inextricably mixed with alchemy and scientific investigation confused with diabolism. Fundamentally writers of this type of story are against change, seeing it as dangerous and destructive; they are diametrically opposed to any form of radical utopianism even though they may often use the same kind of imaginative trappings for their stories. Melmoth's punishment for his experiments and studies is spectacular. Having lived 200 years, having failed to find one person who will agree to his proposition, Melmoth knows he must perish: "No one has ever exchanged destinies with Melmoth the Wanderer. *I have traversed the world in the search, and no one, to gain the world, would lose his own soul!*" He then dreams of his fate:

> His last despairing reverted glance was fixed on the clock of eternity—the upraised black arm seemed to push forward the hand—it arrived at its period—he fell—he sunk—he blazed—he shrieked! The burning waves boomed over his sinking head, and the clock of eternity rung out its awful chime—"Room for the soul of the Wanderer!"—and the waves of the burning ocean answered, as they lashed the adamantine rock—"There is room for more!"—The Wanderer awoke.
> *Melmoth the Wanderer*

Having wakened, the Wanderer discovers he has aged hideously and tells his visitors, "I am summoned, and must obey the summons—my master has other work for me! When a meteor blazes in your atmosphere—when a comet pursues its burning path towards the sun—look up, and perhaps you may think of the spirit condemned to guide the blazing and erratic orb." He warns them that if they watch him leave the house "your lives will be the forfeit of your desperate curiosity. For the same stake I risked more than life—and lost it!" He leaves and terrible shrieks are heard from the nearby cliffs overlooking the sea, indescribable sounds are heard all night over the surrounding countryside. In the morning there is only one trace of the Wanderer on the rocks above the sea—his handkerchief.

Melmoth the Wanderer was published in 1820. Robert Spector in his introduction to *Seven Masterpieces of Gothic Horror* has this to say:

> *Melmoth the Wanderer* is a Faust story that begins in contemporary Ireland but re-creates the adventures of John Melmoth, who has lived since the seventeenth century through a pact with the devil. Through six episodes of terror, Maturin creates the experiences of modern anguish. Maturin combines the myths of Faust and the Wandering Jew with all the horrible episodes of the Gothic romances, and yet he never depends on blood and gore for his effects. What Maturin does is to probe the psychological depths of fear, and, in doing so, he was a little ahead of his audience. Although Melmoth has come to be regarded by many as the masterpiece of terror fiction, it attracted little attention* until psychological Gothicists like Poe and the French Romantics resurrected it some years later.

Throughout this long book Melmoth can also be seen as the Faceless Man of our dreams, the unknown aspect of ourselves which is symbolized as well in the figure of the cowled monk or the shadowy, omniscient spectre. He appears in many modern fantasy tales—Leiber's Sheelba of the Eyeless Face in the "Gray Mouser" stories, Tolkien's faceless villain in the *Lord of the Rings*, Poul Anderson's Odin in *The Broken Sword*, even Alfred Bester's Burning Man in *Tiger! Tiger!* There is a link, too, perhaps, between the unknown aspect and the "evil" aspect of ourselves in that we sense the presence of the unknown aspect and fear it, therefore judging it "evil." Robert Louis Stevenson might have experienced such a process and in *Dr. Jekyll and Mr. Hyde* (1886), inspired by fever-dreams and nightmares during a bad illness, produced a new variant on the Faust-character as Jekyll slowly becomes dominated by Hyde. *The Picture of Dorian Gray* (1891) is another development of the theme. Maturin was an

* See Alethea Hayter's introduction to the Penguin edition for a slightly differ-ent account of the book's success.

ancestor of Wilde's and Wilde changed his name to Sebastian Melmoth when he came out of prison and went to live in Dieppe.

The doomed hero, bound to destroy himself and those he loves, is one of the oldest character-types in literature. Byron saw himself in this role, to the discomfort of his friends and family, and by acting it out helped to foster it in Romantic literature. A good many successful rock and roll performers play a similar role and, as often as not, are destroyed by it, thus giving a semblance of authenticity to the myth. Recent hero-villains in fantastic fiction have been Mervyn Peake's Steerpike in the Gormenghast books, Anderson's Scafloc in *The Broken Sword*, T. H. White's Lancelot in *The Once and Future King* and Jane Gaskell's Zerd in *The Serpent*. Bram Stoker's *Dracula* (1897) is, of course, another variation. Here vampirism is the strongest element in the story, but Count Dracula's lust for blood is almost identical to the lust for virtuous women which marked his predecessors. Faust desired to have and corrupt Margaret, just as dozens of later "demon-lovers" like Radcliffe's Schedoni, Ambrosio and, in real life, Byron and de Sade claimed to pursue innocence solely to destroy it. This peculiar ambition apparently possessed a lot of the great hero-villains. It even seemed to be the secret of their attraction for those refined middle-class women who made up the greatest part of the Gothic's readership and who still comprise the main audience for that degenerated thing, the "Gothic Romance" published by Harlequin and Mills and Boon in huge numbers, not to mention the followers of Anne Rice, who has been as successful with her various vampires as Brontë was with Mr. Rochester..

It would be refreshing, however, to see a few more good hero-villains in modern epic fantasy. Even better would be some full-blooded heroine-villainesses! Their presence might improve a form which is already showing signs of sterility.

2

THE EXOTIC LANDSCAPE

With the sight of those lofty walls and the scent of
the dry sweet sage there rushed over me a strange
feeling that *Riders of the Purple Sage* was true. My
dream people of romance had really lived there once
upon a time. I climbed high upon the huge stones
where Fay Larkin once had glided with swift sure
steps, and I entered the musty cliff-dwellings, and
called out to hear the weird, sonorous echoes, and I
wandered through the thickets and upon the grassy
spruce-shaded benches, never for a moment free of
the story I had conceived there. Something of awe
and sadness abided with me. Surprise Valley seemed
a part of my past, my dreams, my very self. I left it,
haunted by its loneliness and silence and beauty, by
the story it had given me.
Zane Grey, *Tales of Lonely Trails*, 1922

An intrinsic part of the epic fantasy is exotic landscape. This
dream-scenery is fundamental to the success of any romantic
work, from Walpole to Ballard; it is often the substance of
such work, and no matter how well drawn their characters or good
their language writers will appeal to the dedicated reader of romance
according to the skill by which they evoke settings, whether natural
or invented. Their work may be judged not by normal criteria but by
the "power" of their imagery and by what extent their writing evokes

that "power," whether they are trying to convey "wildness", "strangeness" or "charm"; whether, like Melville, Ballard, Juenger, Patrick White or Alejo Carpentier, they transform their images into intense personal metaphors or, like Bunyan, give us simple allegory:

> As I walked through the wilderness of this world, I lighted on a certain place where was a den, and laid me down to sleep; and as I slept, I dreamed a dream. I dreamed, and behold, I saw a man clothed with rags standing in a certain place, a book in his hand, and a great burden on his back.
> *The Pilgrim's Progress*, 1678

The English sf "disaster story," best exemplified by the likes of John Wyndham and J. G. Ballard, was an obvious attempt by authors to remold landscapes to their own literary ends and the device of world-catastrophe proves very useful to them. The central appeal in such books is the landscape, which can be harsh or comfortable, depending on the author's intentions, though often the weight of sf rationalization will collapse the structure and leave only a fragment of the original conception behind, partly because matter-of-fact language and lyrical imagery rarely work to support one another. I discuss elsewhere the appeal of the rural English landscape, the landscape of lost innocence (*à la* Tolkien and his imitators) which derives, I suspect, from the tradition of the pastoral romance (*Arcadia* etc.) through 19th century writers like Borrow, and has modern exponents as varied as Joanna Trollope and Miss Read, but little link with Ann Radcliffe, Clara Reeve, Scott, the Brontës, Stevenson or, for instance, Raymond Chandler, all of whom in different ways imposed an idiosyncratic vision on their scenery. Occasionally, of course, Tolkien manages a romantic evocation or two, passages which are admired by those contemporary readers who do not otherwise enjoy him. But Tolkien's enormous success could easily be in direct relation to the extent to which the elements of romance are *absent* from his narrative. As Fritz Leiber, one of America's leading fantasts, wrote in a letter to Lin Carter,

There's no arguing that a vast number of people…are tremendously and enduringly enthusiastic about Tolkien's trilogy, yet I do meet quite a few whose reactions are much like my own. We almost always start with, "The ents are great! Oh boy, yes. And that first part of the quest with the black riders in the distance and Strider a mystery—that's great, too. And yes, the first appearance of the Nazgul and the Balrog…." At about which point the silence begins and we search our memories and look at each other rather guiltily—exciting things should spring to mind, but they don't…. He's not interested in women and he's not really interested in the villains unless they're just miserable sneaks, bullies and resentful cowards like Gollum…. Tolkien (so unlike Eddison) does not explore and even seems uninterested in exploring the mentality and consciousness and inner life of his chief villains.
1969, quoted in *Imaginary Worlds*
by Lin Carter, 1973

A writer of fantasy must be judged, I think, by the level of inventive intensity at which he or she works. Allegory can be nonexistent but a certain amount of conscious metaphor is always there. The writer who follows such originals without understanding this produces work which is at best superficially entertaining and at worst meaningless on any level—generic dross doing nothing to revitalize the form from which it borrows. A writer's work tends to last in direct ratio to the degree of originality and vitality put into it. Although William Morris is doubtless the originator of the story set in an imaginary land where the supernatural is a fact of life, he borrowed so heavily from Nordic and mediaeval models, in prose, imagery and even characters, that his later writing has little appeal to the modern reader. In his early short prose romances published in the *Oxford and Cambridge Magazine* in 1856 he showed an enthusiasm and vigour generally lacking in his mature work:

> I dreamed once, that four men sat by the winter fire talking and telling tales, in a house that the wind howled around. And one of them, the eldest, said: "When I was a boy, before you came to this land, that bar of red sand rock, which makes a fall in our river, had only just been formed; for it used to stand above the river in a great cliff, tunnelled by a cave about midway between the green-growing grass and the green-flowing river; and it fell one night, when you had not yet come to this land, no, nor your fathers."
>
> *The Dream*

By the end of his life the level of his description was, at its best, usually of this sort:

> It is told that there was once a mighty river which ran south into the sea, and at the mouth thereof was a great and rich city, which had been builded and had waxed and thriven because of the great and most excellent haven which the river aforesaid made where it fell into the sea, and now it was like looking at a huge Wood of barked and smoothened fir-trees when one saw the masts of the ships that lay in the said haven.
>
> *The Sundering Flood*, 1898

The image itself—masts of ships like a forest—is not original and is further marred by the lifeless, imitative prose. A somewhat better writer and the first to follow Morris's example of setting his stories in exotic, invented lands was Lord Dunsany who learned much from Wilde and the aesthetes, from Irish folklorists, poets and dramatists like Yeats and Synge. His prose and his invention is often witty, paradoxical, deriving in part from Oriental fantasies such as those of Beckford, Moore and Burton, and possibly from Doughty's Arabian reminiscences. Like most fantasts he owed a good deal to Thomas de Quincey and Edgar Allan Poe, both in technique and style. De Quincey gives us

The unimaginable horror which these dreams of oriental imagery and mythological tortures impressed upon me...I was stared at, hooted at, grinned at, chattered at, by monkeys, by paroquets, by cockatoos. I ran into pagodas, and was fixed for centuries at the summit, or in secret rooms; I was the idol; I was the priest; I was sacrificed...I came suddenly upon Isis and Osiris: I had done a deed, they said, which the ibis and the crocodile trembled at. Thousands of years I lived and was buried in stone coffins, with mummies and sphinxes, in narrow chambers at the heart of eternal pyramids. I was kissed, with cancerous kisses, by crocodiles, and was laid, confounded with all unutterable abortions, amongst reeds and Nilotic mud.
Confessions of an English Opium Eater, 1822

While from Poe we have the story of "Eleanora" (1840), its narrator dreaming of a past reality more powerful than his present; and of a River of Silence and a Valley of the Many-Coloured Grass:

And, here and there, in groves about this grass, like a wilderness of dreams, sprang up fantastic trees, whose tall slender stems stood not upright, but slanted gracefully towards the light that peered at noon-day into the centre of the valley. Their bark was speckled with the vivid alternate splendour of ebony and silver; and was smoother than all save the cheeks of Eleanora; so that but for the brilliant green of the huge leaves that spread from their summits in long, tremulous lines, dallying with the zephyrs, one might have fancied them giant serpents of Syria doing homage to their sovereign the Sun.

Or from "Shadow—a Parable":

Over some flasks of the red Chian wine, within the walls of a noble hall, in a dim city called Ptolemais, we sat, at night, a company of seven. And to our chamber there was no entrance save by a lofty door of brass: and the door was fashioned by the artisan Corianos, and, being of rare workmanship, was fastened from within. Black draperies, likewise, in the gloomy room, shut out from our view the moon, the lurid stars, and the peopleless streets—but the boding and the memory of Evil; they would not be so excluded.

Dunsany gradually excluded the smell of death as well as the memory of Evil from almost everything he wrote but added humour. The following echoes Poe, yet it is the work of a very different kind of imagination:

> Where the great plain of Tarphet runs up, as the sea in estuaries, among the Cyresian mountains, there stood long since the city of Merimna well-nigh among the shadows of the crags. I have never seen a city in the world so beautiful as Merimna seemed to me when first I dreamed of it. It was a marvel of spires and figures of bronze, and marble fountains, and trophies of fabulous wars, and broad streets given over wholly to the Beautiful.
> *The Sword of Welleran*, 1908

In fact it is much more reminiscent of Wilde in tone. Here is Wilde:

> In the fourth month we reached the city of Illel. It was night time when we came to the grove that is outside the walls, and the air was sultry, for the Moon was travelling in Scorpion. We took the ripe pomegranates from the trees, and brake them, and drank their sweet juices. Then we lay down on our carpets and waited for the dawn. And at dawn we rose and knocked at the gate of the city. It was wrought out of red bronze, and carved with sea-dragons and dragons that have wings. The guards looked down from the battlements and asked us our

business.
"The Fisherman and his Soul," 1888

As with so much fantastic literature the inspiration is from romantic poetry, from *Kubla Khan*, from *Lalla Rookh*, from Keats, from Shelley, from Tennyson and Swinburne. Unfortunately only rarely does the prose ever come to match the best of the poetry. Often the prose is little more than a mindless imitation of the euphonious aspects of the verse which, lacking the substance of the original, takes on the aspect of a mute attempting desperately to sing a Mozart song by mouthing an approximation of the sounds he has heard. All the nonsensical archaicisms and meaningless sonority borrowed from Gothic and Pre-Raphaelite writers used, as often as not, to colour up an essentially lifeless and unimaginative narrative, tends to discredit those few writers, like William Hope Hodgson, who instil vigour and fresh meaning into their language. Hodgson's huge book, which is more nearly a visionary work in the manner of Bunyan than it is a conceit in the manner of Dunsany, is *The Night Land* (1912) which has received some very poor editions over the years but was most recently paperbacked in the generally excellent Victor Gollancz 'Masters of Fantasy' series.

> And afar down the gorge, I did see the shinings of strange fires, faint and a great way off. And so was I come at last to the bottom of the Mighty Slope....
>
> And presently I did go forward again; and so did open the point of the rocks, as the sailors do say. And I saw now that there gushed forth a great blue flame from the earth; and mighty rocks stood about it, as that they were olden giants grouped there to some strange service.
>
> And concerning this flame I was not overmuch astonished in my Reason: for it had seemed to me as I drew anigh, that the fire and the sound should be made by the roaring and whistling of a burning gas that did issue forth among the rocks. Yet, truly, though it did be a natural matter, it was yet a wondrous sight, and set amazement on my senses; for the flame did

dance, and sway whitherward monstrously, and sometimes did seem that it dropt so low as an hundred feet, and afterward went upward with a vast roaring unto the utter height, and did stand mighty and blazing, maybe a full thousand feet, so that the far side of the gorge was lit, and surely it was seven great miles off or more; but yet did show plain and wondrous. And the light did show me the flank of the mountain, that made the right hand side of the Gorge, to go up measureless into the night.

This is archaism used to much livelier effect than Morris's. While the aesthetes were giving us their ornamental style of romance, Kipling was producing, in his Mowgli stories in particular, a style which was to influence a great many of his contemporaries and offer a prevailing voice in the next century. Told simply, yet lyrically, his jungle stories were to influence many American writers, among them Edgar Rice Burroughs whose first fiction was a fantastic romance set on Mars borrowed from Edwin Lester Arnold and Pope's *Journey to Mars* (1894) and in style influenced (perhaps at a stage or two removed) by Kipling and Jack London (whose own *Call of the Wild* owes a great deal to Kipling). This laconic as opposed to lyrical romanticism, with admiration of the naive outsider, the primitive— the unrepressed wish-fulfilment "noble savage" of Victorian fiction— was to be the dominant voice in science fiction and fantasy until relatively recently. Yet it still depended on landscape for much of its appeal. Burroughs created a Mars which was to stimulate the imaginations of a diversity of science fiction writers from Leigh Brackett to Ray Bradbury for the next fifty years :

The quiet of the tomb lay upon the mysterious valley of death, crouching deep in its warm nest within the sunken area at the south pole of the dying planet. In the far distance the Golden Cliffs raised their mighty barrier faces far into the starlit heavens, the precious metals and scintillating jewels that composed them sparkling in the brilliant light of Mars's two gorgeous moons.

At my back was the forest, pruned and trimmed like the sward to parklike symmetry by the browsing of the ghoulish plant men.

Before me lay the Lost Sea of Korus, while farther on I caught the shimmering ribbon of Iss, the River of Mystery, where it would rush out from beneath the Golden Cliffs to empty into Korus, to which for countless ages had been borne the deluded and unhappy Martians of the outer world upon the voluntary pilgrimage to this false heaven.

The Gods of Mars, 1918

Echoes of the Gothic relish for decaying landscape and ruins abound in Burroughs. His "dead sea-bottoms" set the pattern for a fictional Mars, a dying culture on a world almost wholly desert, which many writers were loath to give up, inventing future Earths or planets orbiting faraway stars rather than relinquish such potent images. Burroughs was much influenced by H. Rider Haggard, especially in his Tarzan novels (She-Who-Must-Be-Obeyed and La of Opar are virtually twin sisters), but the American writer to learn most from Haggard and, in my opinion, write better romances, was Abraham Merritt who produced comparatively little work, some of it virtually without any human viewpoint or dramatic tension, but the majority very much linking grotesque and fantastical scenery with a strong adventure element:

There was something about that immense ebon citadel that struck me with the same sense of fore-knowledge that I had felt when I had ridden into the ruins of the Gobi oasis. Also I thought it looked like that city of Dis which Dante had glimpsed in Hades. And its antiquity hung over it like a sable garment.

Then I saw that Nansur was broken. Between the arch that winged from the side on which we stood and the arch that swept up and out from the side of the black citadel, there was a gap. It was as though a gigantic hammer had been swung down on the soaring bow, shattering it at its center. I thought of

Bifrost Bridge over which the Valkyries rode, bearing souls of the warriors to Valhalla; and I thought it had been a great blasphemy to have broken Nansur Bridge as it would have been to have broken Bifrost.
Dwellers in the Mirage, 1932

E. R. Eddison, the British author of *The Worm Ouroboros*, also available in the Fantasy Masterwork series, was perhaps the last to reflect the atmosphere of the previous generation's love for the archaic and the bizarre. He is thought by many to represent the apotheosis of a tradition, a much more witty and original writer than Morris, a rather more original inventor of landscape than Dunsany....

Juss walked long in the doubtful light, troubled at heart.... The glimmer of the lamps mingled with his dreams and his dreams with it, so that scarce he wist whether asleep or waking he beheld the walls of the bedchamber, dispart in sunder, disclosing a prospect of vast paths of moonlight, and a solitary mountain peak standing naked out of a sea of cloud that gleamed white beneath the moon. It seemed to him that the power of flight was upon him, and that he flew to that mountain and hung in air beholding it near at hand, and a circle as the appearance of fire round about it, and on the summit of the mountain the likeness of a bur or citadel of brass that was green with eld and surface-battered by the frosts and winds of ages. On the battlements was the appearance of a great company both men and women, never still, now walking on the wall with hands lifted up as in supplication to the crystal lamps of heaven, now flinging themselves on their knees or leaning against the brazen battlements to bury their faces in their hands, or standing at gaze as night-walkers gazing into the void. Some seemed men of war, and some great courtiers by their costly apparel, rulers and kings and kings' daughters, grave bearded counsellors, youths and maidens and crowned queens. And when

they went and when they stood, and when they
seemed to cry aloud bitterly, all was noiseless even
as the tomb, and the faces of those mourners pallid
as a dead corpse is pallid.
The Worm Ouroboros, 1926

It is a feature of the work of many romantic writers that they
distance themselves in this way. Scott in his *Journal* remarks

I saw the poor child's funeral from a distance. Ah,
that Distance! What a magician for conjuring up
scenes of joy or sorrow, smoothing all asperities,
reconciling all incongruities, veiling all absurdness,
softening every coarseness, doubling every effect by
the influence of the imagination.

It is probably no coincidence that the majority of writers best
known as fantasts, at least until the present couple of generations,
were introverted, reclusive, misanthropic, or that a strong vein of
misogynism built itself into the conventions of the genre over the
years, so that women were unbelievably beautiful goddesses,
treacherous jades or silly slave-girls. Much fantasy was
characteristically bachelor-fiction largely written and read by that
section of the community. Certainly H. P. Lovecraft's unstable
childhood might have turned anyone peculiar and made them seek
escape in Romance. An aggressive, neurotic personality, though not
without his loyalties and virtues, Lovecraft came under the influence
of Poe, Dunsany and the imaginative writers of the Munsey pulp
magazines and produced some of the most powerful infantile
pathological imagery and some of the most astonishingly awful prose
ever to gain popularity, yet his early work, written primarily in homage
to Dunsany, from whom he borrowed the idea of an invented
pantheon of gods, is lighter in touch and almost completely lacking
in the morbid imagery of his more successful horror stories in which
death, idealism, lust and terror of sexual intercourse are constantly
associated in prose which becomes increasingly confused as the
author's embattled psyche received wound after wound and he
regressed into an attitude of permanent defensiveness. The longest

example of this Dunsany phase is *The Dream Quest of Unknown Kadath* (published in book form, 1955).

Clark Ashton Smith was another American recluse who wrote very much under the influence of Poe and Dunsany and had, like Jack Vance, a great influence on M. John Harrison, one of the leading living writers of heroic fantasy. Smith's main career as a writer of short stories, primarily for *Weird Tales*, the pulp which published the bulk of American fantastic fiction from 1923 to 1954, lasted for only six years, in which time he produced nearly a hundred stories, most of them set in invented worlds of the remote past or remote future, some of them on distant planets, all of them exotic. The stories were written with such intensity and control that it is reasonable to guess that Smith burned himself out, perhaps entered a period of depression from which he never completely recovered. Smith's enthusiasm for the Romantics was more literary than most of his contemporaries. He translated Baudelaire and wrote disciplined poetry himself. His prose contains a vitality rarely apparent in this kind of fiction and there is very frequently a strong vein of irony which was to mark the work of a later writer, Fritz Leiber. In Smith intelligence and a genuine love of language, an almost playful relish for the exotic, a carelessness of spirit, in great contrast to the obsessive aggression of Lovecraft, make his work more palatable to me. Just as "distanced," just as suspicious of the world, particularly women, just as morbid in many ways, Smith's stories lack the neurotic drone of writers like Lovecraft, and contain a good deal of ordinary humour. For me, it is his tone which makes him readable where Lovecraft is not:

> Toward night, as the sun declined above that tumultous ebon ocean, it seemed that a great bank of thunder-cloud arose from the west, long and low-lying at first, but surging rapidly skyward with the mountainous domes. Ever higher it loomed, revealing the menace as of piled cliffs and somber, awful seascapes; but its form changed not in the fashion of clouds; and Yadar knew it at last for an island bulking far aloft in the long-rayed sunset. From it a shadow was thrown for leagues, darkening still more the sable

waters, as if with the fall of untimely night; and in the shadow the foam-crests flashing upon hidden reefs were white as the bared teeth of death. And Yadar needed not the shrill frightened cries of his companions to tell him that this was the terrible Isle of Naat.

"Necromancy in Naat," 1936, from *Lost Worlds*

Smith was able to combine rapid action with his descriptions, as Stevenson often did, his landscapes actually contributing to his story's dynamic. In this he had something in common with Robert E. Howard, another reclusive young man who wrote at an enormous rate for a few years before killing himself when his mother's death evidently coincided with a bout of depression resulting from creative exhaustion. Howard wrote pulp adventure stories of every kind, for every market he could find, but his real love was for supernatural adventure and he brought a brash, tough element to the epic fantasy which did much to change the course of the American school away from precious writing and static imagery, just as Hammett, Chandler and the *Black Mask* pulp writers were to change the course of American detective fiction. Howard had no literary ambitions but possessed a vitality his followers never captured. His influences were other pulp writers like Edgar Rice Burroughs, Talbot Mundy, Harold Lamb, Francis Terhune, Abraham Merritt, and his descriptions of interiors and landscapes though rarely very original were intrinsic to the story he was telling. In his Conan stories and his Solomon Kane stories, much more directly influenced by historical novelists in the tradition of Scott and Stevenson, Howard unconsciously produced a remarriage of Gothic and Chivalric traditions in a popular idiom:

The two hosts confronted each other across a wide, shallow valley, with rugged cliffs, and a shallow stream winding through masses of reeds and willows down the middle of the vale. The camp-followers of both hosts came down to this stream for water, and shouted insults and hurled stones across at one another. The last glints of the sun shone on the golden banner of Nemedia with the scarlet dragon, unfurled in the breeze above the pavilion of King Tarascus on an eminence near the eastern cliffs. But the shadow of the western cliffs fell like a vast purple pall across the tents and the army of Aquilonia, and upon the black banner with its golden lion that floated above King Conan's pavilion.

Conan the Conqueror, 1936

Sadly the vitality of the original Conan stories has not been reproduced in the imitations (including films) since done by a variety of hands and Howard's virtues (as a synthesist if nothing else) were threatened with burial as exploitive publishers encouraged further imitations and republished every piece of mediocre work Howard ever wrote. The best of his imitators were contemporaries, who were writing under the same influences.

The movie versions of Conan borrow as many elements from the rest of the genre as they do from Howard, but for me they remain inferior in every way to the originals. The *Star Wars* movies, deriving plot materials from comic books and, among others, Italian Westerns, have had as much influence on these Sword and Sorcery films as anything else. *Hawk the Slayer, The Sword and the Sorcerer* and most of the others have a simple revenge motif as their main dynamic, while almost all have mysteriously missing relatives as the object of a quest. The repetitiveness of the clichés says a great deal, in my view, about the caution and lack of creative originality which infects the film business. The simple minded machismo of the movie Conan is a little like that of the movie Tarzan. All potential is lost. Happily, with the making of the Tolkien books into respectable movie versions, we might hope to see an improvement in the ambition and execution of heroic fantasy films in future. Good directors, surely, can do more with the material, rather than less. We have to hope that the threatened schoolboys who tend to dominate Hollywood and seem only too eager to indulge their fifth-rate fantasies of male violence, will be discouraged as *Lord of the Rings* continues to succeed at the box office. We can only hope that we no longer have to witness a deterioration from the crude, powerful prose of Howard, through the increasingly badly-done comic strip versions, to the feebleness of the movies. The magic fades, its real achievements going unrecognized. One longs for a good film version, say, of Fafhrd and the Gray Mouser, which conceivably might contain dialogue which grown up actors would not be ashamed to speak!

Having no familiarity with Conan at first, influenced by Eddison and Cabell, Fritz Leiber began to publish his Fafhrd and Gray Mouser stories in a short-lived pulp magazine which had ambitions where fantasy was concerned similar to those *Black Mask* had for thrillers. *Unknown* was edited by John W. Campbell, editor of *Astounding Science Fiction*, and was best known for bringing a patina of laconic credibility or "realism" to the fantastic story.

During both world wars much less exotic fantasy was published (and presumably written). Romance had to disguise itself as realism if it was to keep an audience. With the Romantic Revival it had been able to flourish again for a time in its own terms, to disappear for a few decades until the 1960s, when public taste again approved of it—when there was a fresh commercial market which publishers were willing to satisfy. There seemed to be a sharp decline in popular imaginative fantasy around 1914, rising gradually in the mid-twenties and declining again by around 1940, suggesting that during a world war readers have more urgent matters to hold their attention, more important facts to sentimentalize.

Unknown was a magazine for its time when it began in the late thirties and continued into the early war years, publishing some of the most literate popular fantasy ever to appear. Leiber's work was much more evidently romantic than, for instance, Anthony Boucher's (who satirized the werewolf myth in *The Compleat Werewolf*). The majority of *Unknown* writers debunked mythology, folklore and the honor genre. Leiber's Gray Mouser stories were published largely because the characters were more human and "realistic" than any previous characters in this kind of fiction. But Leiber relied as heavily as his predecessors on landscape to create his effects. One story, "The Bleak Shore," was almost as wholly imagist as, say, Stevenson's "The Merry Men." His first Fafhrd and Mouser story was "Adept's Gambit" and here is a characteristic piece of description:

> So they crossed the snowy Lebanons and stole three
> camels, virtuously choosing to rob a rich landlord
> who made his tenants milk rocks and sow the shores

of the Dead Sea, for it was unwise to approach the Gossiper of the Gods with an overly dirty conscience. After seven days of pitching and tossing across the desert, furnace days that made Fafhrd curse Muspelheim's fire gods, in whom he did not believe, they reached the Sand Combers and the Great Sand Whirlpools, and warily slipping past them while they were only lazily twirling, climbed the Rocky Islet. The city-loving Mouser ranted at Ningauble's preference for "a godforsaken hole in the desert," although he suspected that the Newsmonger and his agents came and went by a more hospitable road than the one provided for visitors, and although he knew as well as Fafhrd that the Snarer of Rumors (especially the false, which are the more valuable) must live as close to India and the infinite garden lands of the Yellow Men as to barbaric Britain and marching Rome, as close to the heaven-steaming trans-Ethiopian jungle as to the mystery of lonely tablelands and star-scraping mountains beyond the Caspian Sea.

Although it owes a good deal perhaps to Cabell, it is vastly superior writing to that of Howard or Lovecraft and is marked by Leiber's humane sense of humour. Fletcher Pratt, a collaborator with L. Sprague De Camp in a remarkably funny series of spoofs for *Unknown*, deriving much inspiration from Mark Twain's *A Connecticut Yankee in King Arthur's Court* (1889), admitted the influence of Dunsany as cheerfully as Lovecraft, but his *The Well of the Unicorn* (1948), on rereading a rather plodding affair, bears little trace of any stylistic influences from Pre-Raphaelitism or the Celtic Twilight. It is written in a direct style which, like Leiber and Howard, lacks the "distance" characteristic of the majority of writers before this time and anticipating in this *The Lord of the Rings* for, if it has virtues, it is also remarkable for its failure to employ any form of invented landscape. Its world is Nordic and familiar. The author has no great relish for descriptive writing even of the sort used by Howard. The best we get from Pratt is:

> The wind had risen during the night and under a grey
> sky now carried whorls of snow streaming past the
> windows.

It became unfashionable, even unrespectable, to employ ecstatic language in all but the most lurid of pulps and it was to these that unrepentant romantics looked for publication in the forties and fifties: *Planet Stories* which ran Leigh Brackett's wonderful Eric John Stark stories, *Thrilling Wonder Stories* and *Startling Stories* with Charles Harness. Other shorter-lived magazines featured the occasional Howard pastiche, some Cordwainer Smith, a Leiber story; Jack Vance's *The Dying Earth* was published in a small edition in 1950, Poul Anderson's fine *The Broken Sword* was published in relative obscurity shortly before *The Fellowship of the Ring* in 1954, but it was not until the mid-sixties with the advent of a new, frankly romantic school of sf and fantasy writers associated with the so-called sf new wave that the American magazines were to see a strong revival of public interest in fiction depending more for its success on witty or lyrical writing and evocative landscapes than on "ideas," rationalism and laconic prose. With the renewed success of Burroughs, the cult of Tolkien, the emergence of writers like Zelazny, Delany, Lafferty and Ellison, the tone of generic fantasy (including sf) began to change as a substantial readership developed amongst young people throughout the West. Romantic and mystical writers were revived, together with half-forgotten painters and poets. De Quincey's followers in the so-called drug-culture became legion. A new vogue for the Pre-Raphaelites, for the Aesthetes, the Symbolists, began until today the exotic landscape seems to be predominantly the province of a new school of commercial artists while authors writing in imitation of rediscovered masters like Dunsany and Howard are often content to use prefabricated landscapes. To my knowledge only a few writers now produce epic fantasy which makes conscious literary use of exotic landscape. One of these, M. John Harrison, began experimenting with the form in his *The Pastel City*. His dying world of the far future derives a fair bit from Smith and Vance, owes a trifle to Ballard, but his landscapes illuminate a personal vision:

Dawn broke yellow and black like an omen over the Cobalt-mere, where isolated wreaths of night-mist still hung over the dark, smooth water. From the eyots and reed-beds, fowl cackled: dimly sensing the coming winter, they were gathering in great multicoloured drifts on the surface of the lake, slow migratory urges building to a climax in ten thousand small, dreary skulls.

The Pastel City, 1971

Like Leiber, Harrison is a long way from the oral tradition which so influenced Dunsany, but very much in the literary tradition of Stevenson, and none the worse for that. Moreover, Harrison has developed his work in recent years to arrive at his own specialized kind of fantasy where the epic element exists only in backgrounds, in memories, in ruins, in ancient landscapes and as the *subject matter* of the story itself. He concentrates on the lives of his characters, on the images of their old and threadbare world, on the scenery. What violence is permitted in his stories is shown always as useless, seedy, misconceived, the last resort of despairing fools. Landscape is of paramount importance to Harrison; the landscapes of Viriconium, his antique city, are an indivisible part of the personalities who occupy them. One is reflected in the other. They might even be the same. *A Storm of Wings* (1979) was the second Viriconium book and another advance into Harrison's individual territory. But it was not until *In Viriconium* (1982) that he seemed to break almost completely with any earlier formal influences:

The death and defection of his only allies left him alone in a place he hardly recognised. In one night the plague zone had extended its boundaries by two miles, perhaps three. The High City had succumbed at last. Later he was to write:

"A quiet shabbiness seemed to have descended unnoticed on the squares and avenues. Waste paper blew round my legs as I crossed the empty perspectives of the Atteline Way; the bowls of the everlasting fountains at Delpine Square were dry and dust-filled, the flagstones slippery with birdlime underfoot; insects circled and fell in the orange lamplight along the Camine Auriale. The plague had penetrated everywhere. All evening the salons and drawing rooms of the High City had been haunted by silences, pauses, faux pas: if anyone heard me when I flung myself exhausted against some well-known front door to get my breath it was only as another intrusion, a harsh, lonely sound which relieved briefly the stultified conversation, the unending dinner with its lukewarm sauces and overcooked mutton, or the curiously flat tone of the visiting violinist (who subsequently shook his instrument and complained, 'I find the ambience rather unsympathetic tonight.')

"This psychological disorder of the city was reflected in a new disorder of its streets. It was a city I knew and yet I could not find my way about it...."

Harrison's fantasies increasingly reflect his concern with the origins of our imaginings and why we should need (or want) to create fables and mythologies. In this he shares something in common with a number of modern writers, including Ursula K. Le Guin (see, for instance, *Threshold*, 1980), Robert Holdstock (*Mythago Wood*, 1984) and, as ever, J. G. Ballard who, in this respect, has been an enormous influence on the younger generation of fantasts just as Durrell and Greene can be heard in them all. Most of Ballard's books deal with our relationship to the natural world and the myths we derive from it (*The Drowned World*, 1962, *The Terminal Beach*, 1964, *High Rise*, 1975 and even *Empire of the Sun*, 1984, display this obsession) and while he has not produced anything remotely like an epic fantasy he has been an excellent model for the best of those who have.

Thoracic Drop. The spinal landscape, revealed at the level of T-I2, is that of the porous rock-towers of Tenerife, and of the native of the Canaries, Oscar Dominguez, who created the technique of decalcomania and so exposed the first spinal landscape. The clinker-like rock-towers, suspended above the silent swamp, create an impression of profound anguish. The inhospitability of this mineral world, with its inorganic growths, is relieved only by the balloons flying in the clear sky. They are painted with names: Jackie, Lee Harvey, Malcolm. In the mirror of this swamp there are no reflections. Here, time makes no concessions.

"The Assassination Weapon," 1966

Gene Wolfe, too, has an intellectual fascination with his subject matter, which does not in any way diminish his narrative gift. Of all the writers mentioned, he seems happiest in the long form, but he, too, places great importance on landscape. Wolfe's elegant, deceptively simple and sometimes beautifully ironic style, combined with the originality of his imagination and his outstanding ability as a story teller makes him one of the very best of the generation of fantasts who made their names in the '70s and '80s.

At one point, only slightly less than halfway down, the line of the fault had coincided with the tiled wall of some great building, so that the windy path I trod slashed across it. What the design was those tiles traced, I never knew; as I descended the cliff I was too near to see it, and when I reached the base at last it was too high for me to discern, lost in the shifting mists of the failing river. Yet as I walked, I saw it as an insect may be said to see the face in a portrait over whose surface it creeps. The tiles were of many shapes, though they fit together so closely, and at first I thought them representations of birds, lizards, fish and suchlike creatures, all interlocked in the grip of life. Now I feel that this was not so, that they were instead the shapes of a geometry I failed to comprehend, diagrams so complex that the living forms seemed to appear in them as the forms of actual animals appear from the intricate geometries of complex molecules.

The Sword of the Lictor, 1982

Even that enjoyable comic spoof of the Sword and Sorcery genre, Terry Pratchett's *The Colour of Magic* (1983), continues to place strong emphasis on landscape, as here:

> On either side of him two glittering curtains of water hurled towards infinity as the sea swept around the island on its way to the long fall. A hundred yards below the wizard the largest sea salmon he had ever seen flicked itself out of the foam in a wild, jerky and ultimately hopeless leap. Then it fell back, over and over, in the golden underworld light.
>
> Huge shadows grew out of that light like pillars supporting the roof of the universe. Hundreds of miles below him the wizard made out the shape of something, the edge of something—
>
> Like those curious little pictures where the silhouette of an ornate glass suddenly becomes the outline of two faces, the scene beneath him flipped into a whole, new terrifying perspective. Because down there was the head of an elephant as big as a reasonably-sized continent. One mighty tusk cut like a mountain against the golden light, trailing a widening shadow towards the stars. The head was slightly tilted, and a huge ruby eye might almost have been a red supergiant that had managed to shine at noonday. Below the elephant—
>
> Rincewind swallowed and tried not to think—
>
> Below the elephant there was nothing but the distant, painful disc of the sun. And, sweeping slowly past it, was something that for all its city-sized scales, its crater-pocks, its lunar cragginess, was indubitably a flipper.

The inseparability between human beings and their myths is as constant a theme in epic fantasy as is our oneness with nature. Many of the writers emphasize the existence of a deep bond between humans and their world. It is the persistent element in a large proportion of modern work. Here is Patricia A. McKillip:

He left the City of Circles that evening and spent days and nights he did not count, hidden from the world and almost from himself, within the land-law of Heron. He drifted shapelessly in the mists, seeped down into the still, dangerous marshlands, and felt the morning frost silver his face as it hardened over mud and reeds and tough marsh grasses. He cried a marsh bird's lonely cry and stared at the stars out of an expressionless slab of stone. He roamed through the low hills, linking his mind to rocks, trees, rivulets, searching into the rich mines of iron and copper and precious stones the hills kept enclosed within themselves. He spun tendrils of thought into a vast web across the dormant fields and lush, misty pastureland, linking himself to the stubble of dead roots, frozen furrows, and tangled grasses the sheep fed on. The gentleness of the land reminded him of Hed, but there was a dark, restless force in it that had reared up in the shapes of tors and monoliths.
Harpist in the Wind, 1979

The landscape and its inhabitants are seen very much as a unity in Holdstock's *Mythago Wood*. Indeed the subject of the story is this unity and the unity of our dreams with our environment. Apparently drawing from influences as diverse as *The Golden Bough*, Arthur Machen and modern anthropology, *Mythago Wood* makes powerful use of its materials, reinforming them and proving, as always, that a subject is never dead in the hands of an inspired and original author. It has something in common with Le Guin's *Threshold* (*The Beginning Place* in its US edition), which suggests that the imagined world is somehow connected with the wish-fulfilment or personalities of her young characters (her book is a juvenile), but I can think of no story I have read in recent years which so successfully invokes the mystery and magic of the wildwood. Thematically it has something in common with George Meredith's excellent (and also analytical) poem *The Woods of Westermaine*. If the book's resolution leaves something to be desired, this is doubtless because other volumes are planned.

Keeton said the words that I knew to be true: "The whole building is a mythago. And yet it means nothing to me…"

The lost broch. The ruined place of stone, fascinating to the minds of men who lived below steep thatch, inside structures of wicker and mud. There could be no other explanation.

And indeed, the broch marked the outskirts of an eerie and haunting landscape of such legendary, lost buildings.

The forest felt no different, but as we followed animal paths and natural ridges through the bright undergrowth, so we could see the walls and gardens of these ruined, abandoned structures. We saw an ornately gabled house, its windows empty, its roof half-collapsed. There was a Tudor building of exquisite design, its walls grey-green with mossy growth, its timbers corroded and crumbling. In its garden, statues rose like white marble wraiths, faces peering at us from the tangle of ivy and rose, arms outstretched, fingers pointing.

In one place the wood itself changed subtly, becoming darker, more pungent. The heavy predominance of deciduous trees altered dramatically. Now a sparsely foliaged pine-forest covered the descending slope of the land.

The air felt rarefied, sharp with the odour of the trees. And we came at once upon a tall wooden house, its windows shuttered, its tiled roof bright. A great wolf lay curled in the glade that surrounded it: a bare garden, not grassy but heavy with pine needles, and dry as a bone. The wolf smelled us and rose to its feet, raising its muzzle and emitting a haunting, terrifying cry.

Mythago Wood, 1984

It is the processes of imaginative invention which fascinate so many of these newer writers. Yet they have a great deal in common with their predecessors. Where Walpole celebrated "Gothick" ruins, decaying woodlands and antique vistas, in common with so many 18th century romantics, writers like Harrison and Wolfe maintain their romance with ancient stones by describing an Earth of the distant future. Wolfe, in his relish for the idea of our planet in her senility, has a way of revealing his landscapes piece by piece, of adding one extra element at a time so that eventually you realize how vast or bizarre the scene is. This matter-of-fact method (which has 18th century models) plus the introduction of unexplained words (most of which also seem to be useful archaicisms rather than neologisms) is what helps lend atmosphere to his stories. Where Harrison leaves things unsaid or unexplained, Wolfe deliberately adds mystery by providing an off-hand description which merely raises more questions.

It seems significant to me that the majority of the writers who have closely followed Tolkien have not produced much in the way of original landscape. Deserts and mountains are vast and forests are dense. In the work of people like Stephen Donaldson (who claims Conrad and James as his masters) they are rarely more than Hollywood movie scenery. Here, Donaldson's hero Thomas Covenant (whose only virtue is his scepticism about the "reality" of the world he inhabits) describes how his world came to be created:

> Even to himself, his voice sounded bodiless, as if the dark were speaking for him. He was trying to reach out to her with words, though he could not see her, and had no very clear idea of Who she was. His tale was a simple one; but for him its simplicity grew out of long distillation. It made even his dead nerves yearn as if he were moved by an eloquence he did not possess.
>
> In the measureless heavens of the universe, he told her, where life and space were one, and the immortals strode through an ether without limitation, the Creator looked about him, and his heart swelled with the desire to make a new thing to gladden his bright children. Summoning his strength and subtlety,

he set about the work which was his exaltation.

First he forged the Arch of Time, so that the world he wished to make would have a place to be. And then within the Arch he formed the Earth. Wielding the greatness of his love and vision as tools, he made the world in all its beauty, So that no eye could behold it without joy. And then upon the Earth he placed all the myriads of its inhabitants—beings to perceive and cherish the beauty which he made. Striving for perfection because it was the nature of creation to desire all things flawless, he made the inhabitants of the Earth capable of creation, and striving, and love for the world.

Then he withdrew his hand and beheld what he had done.

The Wounded Land, 1980

A relish for what is old, ruined, time-worn, is as prevalent in modern epic fantasy as it was in the Gothic of the late 18th century:

But the keep was still quite solid, thick-walled enough so that an earthquake could hardly have brought it down. There were no windows but arrowslits, the tower top was deeply crenellated, and the door was of iron a foot thick, judging by the fact that it had not rusted away in all the intervening years. Time had been kind to the place. Its mortar had grown stronger with age, and only here or there was any stone shattered by frost. It was a redoubt worthy of the name, and it stood there at the center of the cuplike vale with stolid rocky patience, frowning at the surrounding hills, antique and indomitable.

Diane Duane, *The Door into Fire*, 1979

She grew tall and strong in the Mountain wildness, with her mother's slender bones and ivory hair and her father's black, fearless eyes. She cared for the animals, tended the garden, and learned early how to hold a restless animal against its will, how to send an ancient name out of the silence of her mind, to probe into hidden, forgotten places. Ogam, proud of her quickness, built a room for her with a great dome of crystal, thin as glass, hard as stone, where she could sit beneath the colors of the night world and call in peace. He died when she was sixteen, leaving her alone with the beautiful white house, a vast library of heavy, ironbound books, a collection of animals beyond all dreaming, and the power to hold them.

She read one night not long afterward, in one of his oldest books, of a great white bird with wings that glided like snowy pennants unfurled in the wind, a bird that had carried the only Queen of Eldwold on its back in days long before. She spoke its name softly to herself: Liralen; and, seated on the floor beneath the dome, with the book still open in her lap, she sent a first call forth into the vast Eldwold night for the bird whose name no one had spoken for centuries.
Patricia A. McKillip, *The Forgotten Beasts of Eld*, 1980

Green hills, green wood and a bright river that ran down a gorge to what had been dead sea-bottom but was now—sea. And down on that far sunlit coast he saw the glitter of a white city. Jekkara, bright and strong between the verdant hills and the mighty ocean, that ocean that had not been seen upon Mars for nearly a million years.
Leigh Brackett, *The Sword of Rhiannon*, 1953

And so on. Leigh Brackett's Matt Carse, whose adventures were on Mars, might as easily have been a hero of epic fantasy. He had all the right impulses:

"I have come into the past of Mars. All my life I have studied and dreamed of the past. Now I am in it. Matthew Carse, archaeologist, renegade, looter of tombs."

Leigh Brackett's Mars was heavily influenced by Edgar Rice Burroughs's, but her descriptions of the planet's ancient landscapes were, in my opinion, far more evocative of a sense of magical reality and were to become a strong influence on the young Ray Bradbury.

This fascination with the antique is combined, of course, with a preference for archaic style. Most of the current attempts at this sort of "high" English are pretty pathetic, reminiscent of children trying to write historical stories by peppering the text with phrases like "shiver me timbers." They borrow largely from Tolkien as usual and produce from his original porridge a gruel increasingly thin and lumpy. Lacking even the schoolmasterly sarcasm and irony of a Chesterton, these imitations are about as valuable, in literary terms, as a faded print of *The Hay Wain*. They are moulded from the basest of metals. They are like mass-produced ikons. They are the literary equivalents of the painted plaster saints and statuettes of Christ found in any Lourdes supermarket, or like those toys produced in their thousands in China and Russia. They are actually made by individuals, but there is virtually no evidence for this. One longs for the crisp, well-written sentences of, say, Mary Stewart:

> From this flowery and winding tract of green the land rises towards the north to rolling moorland, where, under the windy stretches of sky, sudden blue lakes wink in the sun. In winter it is a bleak country, where wolves and wild men roam the heights, and come sometimes over-close to the houses; but in summer it is a lovely land, with forests full of deer, and fleets of swans sailing the waters. The air over the moors sparkles with bird-song, and the valleys are alive with skimming swallows and the bright flash of kingfishers. And along the edge of the whinstone runs the Great Wall of the Emperor Hadrian, rising and dipping as the rock rises and dips. It commands the country from its long cliff-top, so that from any point of its fold upon fold of blue distance fades away east or westward, till the eye loses the land in the misty edge of the sky.
>
> *The Last Enchantment*, 1979

And yet a matter-of-fact style can also produce some peculiar effects as in Jane Gaskell's work:

> After two days of rain the little gullies are no longer gullies but the rocky channels of rushing, gurgling, obstreperous streams. The little crops are beaten and drenched but they are of grains anciently mountain-bred and are not spoilt. They have obviously suffered more from the desultory ravages made upon them by the army before me. I suppose it was quashed wherever possible; the despoilers might even have been executed; but on the whole I think the Northern army can get away with some living off the country here. Amiability is at such a low ebb between the Northerners and the Southerners that it can scarcely be worsened—and we do, I mean the Northerners do, to some extent hold the whip hand because we know how to un-vacuum vacuums.
>
> *The Serpent*, 1963

For a far better discussion of the problems of style in epic fantasy, as well as an excellent discussion of the nature of the form, I recommend Ursula K. Le Guin's frequently reprinted essay "From Elfland to Poughkeepsie" (in *The Language of the Night*, 1978) which also appears in a collection of essays on the subject of fantasy by writers most usually identified with fantasy, *Fantasists on Fantasy* edited by Robert H. Boyer and Kenneth J. Zahorski (Avon Books, 1984).

It seems to me that not enough modern practitioners pay sufficient attention to the invention of their own specific landscapes: landscapes which reflect the themes of the stories, amplify or at least complement the moods of the characters, give added texture and apt symbolism to the narratives. There is a great deal of self-indulgence, I believe, amongst those who try to emulate the great writers of fantasy. Too many younger authors fail to realize that quite as much discipline is required to create a good fantasy tale as to make any other kind of good story. Attention to landscape, as a specific means of clarifying, heightening or counter-pointing a fantasy story, is frequently ignored completely. "Mighty" deserts and "gloomy" forests make for reading which is as dull as the worst of the decadent romances, the goblin stories of third-rate *Stürm & Drangers* or a bad Gothic tale. Descriptive language does not have to be particularly complex or lyrical to work; but it does have to have clarity and freshness. One of the best of the newer epic fantasy writers, who has used the form successfully to reflect her own feminism without once failing to tell a good story, is Elizabeth A. Lynn, a writer who effectively employs a contemporary style in her tales of high adventure:

> The Ismenin house was made of stone. It sat on a bluff, with its broad back to the river. It was new. The original Ismenin mansion, like the other great houses of the city, had been built of red cypress, that beautiful wood which had the property of silvering as it aged. It was Rath Ismenin, Ron Ismenin's grandfather, who had caused the stone house to be built. In the Council Year Ninety-Three, he and others traveled to Tezera, to discuss the effects of the Ban on commerce. Visiting the high families of Tezera, Rath Ismenin walked through marble halls for the first time. When he returned south, he ordered the Ismenin mansion razed to the earth, and built himself a house of white granite, with architects and masons hired from Tezera, under the shocked gaze of his neighbors.
> *The Northern Girl*, 1980

Another writer who has used contemporary English successfully in his fantasy is Colin Greenland:

> Dubilier woke. There was light, though the fire had long since shrunk to a mound of cold ash. It was the moon, pouring in through empty window-frames. He put his blanket over his shoulders and went outside.
> The ruins shone silver, white and jet. The magic rays stripped off the daylight shapes and revealed the skeletal forms of a lunar world. Streets and houses

became dry gulleys and grottos; a sagging wall and a pile of bricks turned back into a ragged outcrop and a scree slope beneath. Stalagmites and craters broke the plane of a ravaged plateau. He saw the ten thousand ghosts who thronged the canyons and lingered on the doorsteps of the caves. Their race was new to him: men and women with protuberant eyes, large hands, large hips. They welcomed him. Among them were a few of a different breed, long-necked, lobeless, emphatically erect, like the portraits of ancestors in the galleries of Thryn. They seemed to be gathering around him, pushing themselves to the front of the crowd. We are the road-makers, they said, but you are the greatest builder of all. Perfection on you, master, they hailed him, their parched voices like the wind in dead trees. Ibne, Aigu. Not me, he said. I'm—

He ran. They didn't follow. He came to the road. How could that be the same thing as the broken one they'd slept on, their first night in the marshes? That was a world away; this was a broad road on the moon. From here it drove straight ahead for miles, then plunged and twisted through the jumbled foothill country, lost to sight. Perhaps it reached the mountains. The moonlight turned brick to rock; rock it sublimated, rendering it pure crystal. Hisper Einou loomed above them all, a flawless diamond. Somewhere on those glassy slopes. He was like a pilgrim in an old romance, sent by his lady to fetch an impossible treasure from the lap of a jealous god.
Daybreak on a Different Mountain, 1984

Greenland is also a writer whose work contains elements of analysis. The subject matter of romance is often the chief thematic material of these stories. Greenland, like Harrison, first made his name as a critic of fantasy and science fiction. It is possible to detect in both writers a certain amount of self-consciousness, absent in most of those who went before them. If this sometimes demands new ways of story-telling, it certainly makes for improved writing. Here is Harrison again:

> The aristocratic thugs of the High City whistle as they go about their factional games among the derelict observatories and abandoned fortifications at Lowth. Distant or close at hand, these exchanges—short commanding blasts and protracted responses which often end on what you imagine is an interrogative note—form the basis of a complex language, to the echo of which you wake suddenly in the leaden hour before dawn. Go to the window: the street is empty. You may hear running footsteps, or a sigh. In a minute or two the whistles have moved away in the direction of the Tinmarket or the Margarethestrasse. Next day some minor prince is discovered in the gutter with his throat cut, and all you are left with is the impression of secret wars, lethal patience, an intelligent manoeuvring in the dark.
>
> The children of the Quarter pretend to understand these signals. They know the histories of all the most desperate men in the city. In the mornings on their way to the Lycee on Simeonstrasse they examine every exhausted face.
>
> "Viriconium Knights," *Viriconium Nights*, 1985

This collection of stories about Viriconium is the most recent of Harrison's fantasy books I have read. In it he has produced some of his very best work to date. In spite of a tendency to repeat himself, in common with other writers of his intensive, autobiographical and elliptical methods, he remains one of our finest and most sophisticated imaginative writers, playing with form as he plays with it in his recent science fantasy *Light*. "A Young Man's Journey To Viriconium," for instance, has rather a lot in common with the author's earlier "Egnaro," and was probably best retitled "A Young Man's Journey to London" in later collections. This more recent work is that of a prose stylist considerably superior to almost anyone else working within this genre. Harrison does have a tendency to repeat the effects of authors he greatly admires. His homages to the likes of Colette, T. S. Eliot, H. E. Bates and so on may be discovered in almost everything he has written, but the work is none the worse for that. Most recently, however, his admiration for his own writing tends to produce a sense of *déjà vu* which is perhaps not always intentional and moreover tends to emphasize the streak of misanthropism which runs through a great deal of this kind of fiction. It would be a great shame if such talent came to be spoiled by its author turning too much in on himself.

Whatever minor weaknesses Harrison has, he remains the outstanding fantast of his generation.

> Deserts spread to the north-east of the city, and in a wide swathe to its south.
>
> They are of all kinds, from peneplains of disintegrating metallic dust—out of which rise at intervals lines of bony incandescent hills—to localised chemical sumps, deep, tarry and corrosive, over whose surfaces glitter small flies with papery wings and perhaps a pair of legs too many. These regions are full of old cities which differ from Vriko only in the completeness of their deterioration. The traveller in them may be baked to death; or, discovered with his eyelids frozen together, leave behind only a journal which ends in the middle of a sentence.
>
> The Metal Salt Marches, Fenlen Island, the Great Brown Waste: the borders of regions as exotic as this are drawn differently on the maps of competing authorities: but they are at least bounded in the conventional sense. Allmans Heath, whose borders can be agreed by everyone, does not seem to be. Neither does it seem satisfactory now to say that while those deserts lie outside the city, Allmans Heath lies within it.
>
> "The Dancer from the Dance," *Viriconium Nights*

Perhaps more thoroughly than any of his contemporaries, Harrison understands the value of landscape to his stories. His precise evocation of crucial images acts together with the narrative's other elements, with his characters, both to intensify and complement the story. Perhaps the fact that Harrison reads very little epic fantasy and looks to the likes of Elizabeth Taylor and Turgenev for models rather than to his immediate peers offers some explanation for his success in this genre. Too frequently one gets the impression that, as with the world of science fiction, most practitioners of epic fantasy read only one another's work, a little bit of the latest phat phantasy and, perhaps, rather too much Professor Tolkien. Harrison and those who have been influenced by him to find their own paths, are to be applauded. Standards are higher for their existence.

3
THE HEROES AND HEROINES

My good blade carves the casques of men,
My tough lance thrusteth sure,
My strength is as the strength of ten,
Because my heart is pure.
The shattering trumpet shrilleth high,
The hard brands shiver on the steel,
The splinter'd spear-shafts crack and fly,
The horse and rider reel:
They reel, they roll in clanging lists,
And when the tide of combat stands,
Perfume and flowers fall in showers,
That lightly rain from ladies' hands.
　Tennyson, *Sir Galahad*

Inspired by Macpherson's spurious Celtic "Ossian" ballads which were to give huge impetus to the whole idea of Celtic Romanticism, inspired by Percy's *Reliques*, by Gothic romances, Scott created a form of historical fiction which has scarcely changed. He gave us all sorts of hesitant heroes and noble villains (as well as more interesting minor characters) and probably did most to promote the Victorian stereotype of the "decent chap" in popular fiction. Although in antique costume, his heroes (like Tennyson's) with their stolid nobility, their sense of right and wrong, their honest simplicity, lack only a battered briar and a disreputable Norfolk to be everything the right sort of Wodehousian (or maybe Whitean) Englishman should be. For all that Scott at his best, and later Stevenson (fulfilling Scott's early promise), could frequently offer a witty perspective on such characters, it is usually true of imitations that they borrow all the superficial ideas while failing to understand the irony which almost invariably gives a book lasting qualities.

For the most part H. Rider Haggard, Conan Doyle and others continued the "decent chap" tradition in romances set not only in remote historical periods but in remote lands beyond the fringes of the Empire. Allan Quatermain, Haggard's greatest hero, was decent about almost everything except "sham" and "wanton cruelty," even when travelling mystically in Time. Quatermain's death, in the lost land of Zu-Vendi, was recorded in the book which contains his "portrait" and bears his name:

> And so, a few minutes before sunset, on the third night after his death, they laid him on the brazen flooring before the altar, and waited for the last ray of the setting sun to fall upon his face. Presently it came, and struck him like a golden arrow, crowning the pale brows with glory, and then the trumpets blew, and the flooring revolved, and all that remained of our beloved friend fell into the furnace below.
>
> We shall never see his like again if we live a hundred years. He was the ablest man, the truest gentleman, the firmest friend, the finest sportsman, and, I believe, the best shot in all Africa.
>
> And so ended the very remarkable and adventurous life of Hunter Quatermain.
> *Allan Quatermain*, 1887

Quatermain, like many others, was effectually revived in still stranger tales like *The Ancient Allan* (1919) and *She and Allan* (1926), and in some ways Allan's life was only just beginning as he was reincarnated under other names by subsequent authors, just as Ayesha (She) herself was to become the quintessential heroine-villainess of a thousand lost land adventures.

In this kind of fiction gentlemen heroes were the rule: John Carter (the "gentleman of Virginia"), Tarzan (in his Lord Greystoke persona), Merritt's protagonists—all decent chaps, usually assisted by admiring noble savages. Quatermain had the Zulu Chief Umslopogaas (himself in line of direct descent from Chingachgook, the Last of the Mohicans), Carter had Tars Tarkas, the green Martian prince. These were all characters who could utter the philosophy which, for reasons of reticence and good breeding, the central characters could not. They were full of simple words of wisdom about the horrors of civilization which they delivered in dignified, sometimes archaic speech. Noble savages to a man.

Hawkeye was essentially in the same mould as Scott's characters but superficially "wilder"—more evidently alienated and suspicious of the world and the prototype for almost every Western hero who followed him. He was also an ancestor of Mowgli and Tarzan.

Although Burroughs claimed never to have been influenced by the Mowgli stories (Kipling complained of his imitations) there are too many similarities for this to be absolutely credible. In style, in development, in everything but detail and plot they are alike. Certainly there is also a strong hint of Fenimore Cooper in the fundamentally 19th century style of Burroughs, but Kipling is always present. The simple language of the primitive used to give weight and dignity to simplified ideas about the Law of the Jungle, the nobility of the beast over Man and so on, also occurs in Jack London and has echoes (the use is very different) in Wells. *Jungle Tales of Tarzan*, considered by many to include Burroughs's best writing, is without question an imitation of *The Jungle Book*. But Kipling and Burroughs were probably the first writers to make the Noble Savage the central character in their stories (though Mary Shelley's Monster is an ancestor). Previously the savages had always been sidekicks—in Scott, Cooper, Melville, Lew Wallace they are there to castigate the over-sophisticated modern world and to die touching deaths. They take the place of the Fool or Jester whose function was often similar in Shakespeare, Scott (*Ivanhoe* gives us both types) Dumas (*Chicot the Jester* may be the first hero of his kind in historical fiction) and Hugo. It was not until the beginning of the 20th century, however, that the noble savage began regularly to serve as a protagonist rather than as a foil.

When Umslopogaas, no longer dependent on a father figure, learning a new kind of self-respect, ditches Allan Quatermain and becomes Conan it is Quatermain who becomes the wondering sidekick, the gentleman "dude" of the Westerns who, in turn, dies a good and fairly noble death. Chingachgook becomes Burroughs's *Apache Devil* (1933). If Queequeg is Hiawatha in revolt then Chief Sequoya (Bester's *The Computer Connection*, 1975) is Queequeg triumphant.

Mutable history suited the romantic story-tellers while it was possible to see the past as delicious and misty, but rigorous scholarship, closer proximity, faster travel and Edwardian scepticism forced them abroad to India, Africa, China, or into parallel worlds or Earthlike planets where Scott's carping Doctor Driasdust could be left far behind, where unpalatable imagination-curbing facts simply hadn't occurred—where the Red Man still held sway over North America, or an easily understood mediaeval utopia could be found on Mars, or a great, exotic civilization could exist "before the Flood." Even in the Western the romantic spirit maintained itself, but only because it took on, like the thriller, a patina of realism with Max Brand, Clarence E. Mulford and Zane Grey continuing the spirit of the dime novel while pretending to dispense hard facts and, as often happens, virtually creating a modern West prepared to go to almost any lengths to support its own myth. The frankly romantic story became primarily fantastic with Burroughs, Merritt and George Allan England in the pulps and with Dunsany, Eddison and Hodgson elsewhere. It was not, in fact, until the great success of *The Lord of the Rings*—almost a modern "Ossian"—that the form again came into its own, with the beginning of the 1960s revival of interest in Romantic movements in the arts.

Robert E. Howard was never a commercially successful writer in his lifetime. His brash, hasty, careless style did not lend itself even to the classier pulps. Most of his work appeared in the cheapest of them. The best was published in *Weird Tales*. Howard seems to be the first fantast to make a noble savage (or at least a sceptical barbarian) the central character of an epic fantasy. Quatermain was always an interloper, an observer of the worlds he visited. Conan was integral to his ancient "pre-historic" Hyperborea and yet much more "alienated" than Quatermain, aggressively contemptuous of Quatermain's values (though not, however, the fascist of the movies).

If the form of Howard's stories was borrowed at third and fourth hand from Scott and Fenimore Cooper, the supernatural element from Poe and others, the barbarian hero of the Conan stories owed a great deal to Tarzan and other Burroughs primitives. Given to impulsive violent action, sudden rough affection and bouts of melancholy, Conan was a sort of pint-sized King Kong. Conan mistrusted civilization. He was forever at odds both with the respectable world and the occult world; forever detecting plots to seduce him. Looking back over his life, when King of Aquilonia, he was able to feel regret for his old, free existence:

> "I saw again the battlefield whereon I was born," said Conan, resting his chin moodily on a massive fist. "I saw myself in a pantherskin loin-clout, throwing my spear at the mountain beasts. I was a mercenary swordsman again, a hetman of the *kosaki* who dwell along the Zaporoska River, a corsair looting the coasts of Kush, a pirate of the Barachan Isle, a chief of the Himelian hillmen. All these things I've been, and of all these things I dreamed; all shapes that have been *I* passed like an endless procession, and their feet beat out a dirge in the sounding dust...."
> *Conan the Conqueror*, 1936

This passage also gives us a clue to many of Howard's influences. He did not bother to rationalize or disguise the different lands and cultures of his Hyperborean world. Anachronisms are everywhere. If Scott could make errors involving a few years or a couple of hundred miles, Howard's hero spanned several thousand years of history and thousands of miles. It is as if Conan is trapped in a movie studio, or a movie library of old clips, shifting from 17th century Russia, to Rome in the first century B.C., to 19th century Afghanistan, to the Spanish Main of the 18th century, to the Court of Lorenzo the Magnificent, all the way back to the Stone Age. This mélange of influences was scarcely digested before Howard was, as it were, pouring it back onto the page. It was the personality of Conan— moody, savage, boyish in his loyalties and his treatment of girls— which bound all this stuff together and made the stories somehow credible. If Conan was a projection of Howard's fantasy self, he was a very successfully-realized one and a refreshing change from

Lovecraft's self-involved neurotics.

The Conan stories appeared in *Weird Tales* until 1936. With their popularity a variety of writers was encouraged to submit similar stories to the magazine. Catherine L. Moore was probably the best of these. Her female protagonist Jirel of Joiry was an amazon driven to martial and occult practices in order to avenge her wrongs (she had first appeared in *Weird Tales* in 1933). The locale of the stories was a kind of mythical French kingdom, not a million miles from Cabell's Poictesme. The stories had all of Howard's drive, were rather better written and certainly more consistent.

> She came out into the torchlight, stumbling with exhaustion, her mouth scarlet from the blood of her bitten lip and her bare greaved legs and bare sword-blade foul with the deaths of those little horrors that swarmed around the cavemouth. From the tangle of red hair her eyes stared out with a bleak, frozen inward look, as of one who had seen nameless things. That keen, steel-bright beauty which had been hers was as dull and fouled as her sword-blade, and at the look in her eye Father Gervasse shuddered and crossed himself.
> *Shambleau*, 1953

Almost all romantic heroes and heroines are wounded children (including *King Kong* and *Frankenstein)*, which is perhaps why so many juvenile fantasies are enjoyed by admirers of Tolkien and Howard. Until relatively recently, very few adult central characters existed in pure "sword and sorcery" stories—they are either permanent adolescents, like Conan, actual children like Ged in Ursula Le Guin's *Wizard of Earth Sea*, youths like Airar Alvarson in *The Well of the Unicorn*, or quasi-children like the hobbits in *The Lord of the Rings*. Harry Potter's success depends, for good or ill, on the age at which he began his studies and the Pullman trilogy would have been a very different set of books if the heroine had been a grownup. Innocent, sensitive, intensely loyal and enthusiastic, given to sudden tantrums and terrors, impressionable, sentimental and sometimes ruthless, these characters rarely show mature human responses to their environment, their fellow creatures or the problems they face. They may often do something noble, self-sacrificing or very brave—as *children*—by facing evil down or telling the truth in spite of danger (Alan Garner's *Elidor*, Susan Cooper's *The Dark is Rising*) and doubtless these are worthwhile lessons to childish intellects (for moral lessons of some sort are still present in most children's fiction of this kind: E. Nesbit, *The Hobbit*, the Narnia books and so on). Savages and naïve barbarians often substitute for actual children in popular fiction. The pretend-adults like Conan might claim adult motives—simple greed, sexual lust, calculated vengeance—but emotionally they are pre-pubescent. Even the cynical characters are cynics of the order of Vernon-Smythe (the Cad of Greyfriars School, the emotional epicentre of Hogworts) and it is very rare to find any sort of real grown-up in epic fantasy (a case could be made against Cabell or Kurt Vonnegut for their relentless universal ironies, cumbersome signals, which often have the distinct echo of the schoolroom pedant. *Shangri-la* written by *Mr. Chips. The Collected Fantasies of Miss Jean Brodie*).

Partially, of course, we know that genre demands influence an author in his or her choice of character. It is often useful to have a naïf as the wondering centre of the story; partially, however, the form itself displays a rejection of adult responsibility and of any sort of sophisticated humanity. Only when T. H. White shifts the emphasis of his story of *The Once and Future King* to the adult concerns of his characters does the book reveal its tragic core, which can be seen as a melancholy description of that very process of translation from idealistic youth to humane maturity as the characters reluctantly face the onset of puberty and the implications of their own actions; satisfying the cruel demands of their faith.

A few years after Howard's death, Fritz Leiber began to write his tales of Fafhrd and the Gray Mouser, beginning with the already mentioned "Adept's Gambit" (which was not published until 1947). Though my guess is that they have their spiritual origins in the films of Douglas Fairbanks (*The Three Musketeers*, *Robin Hood*, *The Thief of Baghdad*, *The Gaucho*) and Curtiz-Flynn talkies like *Robin Hood* and *The Sea Hawk*, as well as books, these are unquestionably the most mature and skilful stories to be written consciously as generic epic fantasy or "sword-and-sorcery" (Leiber's original phrase for this sort of fiction). They are rogue's tales borrowing a fair amount from James Branch Cabell, something from E. R. Eddison, and something from good historical and occult fiction, but they are written by a very talented and original writer, one of the most talented fantasts America has known. Like his friend Bradbury, Leiber was one of the few writers of science fiction, for instance, to have any real understanding of language or passionate familiarity with good prose and poetry. Ironist, parodist, satirist, Leiber was consistently ahead of his time in the commercial magazines he contributed to and has a record of his work being "discovered" by a large audience sometimes decades after it first appeared. The Fafhrd and Gray Mouser stories rarely contain a wrong note, are full of ironic metaphor, and, significantly, the Gray Mouser is unquestionably an adult hero (though with adolescent weaknesses), the most original to appear in fantasy fiction. Here are the two described by Leiber in his introduction to *The Swords of Lankhmar* (1968):

> In Fafhrd and the Mouser are rogues through and through, though each has in him a lot of humanity and at least a diamond chip of the spirit of true adventure. They drink, they feast, they wench, they brawl, they steal, they gamble, and surely they hire out their swords to powers that are only a shade better, if that, than the villains. It strikes me (and something might be made of this) that Fafhrd and the Gray Mouser are almost at the opposite extreme from the heroes of Tolkien. My stuff is at least equally as fantastic as his, but it's an earthier sort of fantasy with a strong seasoning of "black fantasy"—or of black humor, to use the current phrase for something that was once called gallows humor and goes back a long, long way. Though with their vitality, appetites, warm sympathies and imagination, Fafhrd and the Mouser are anything but "sick" heroes.
>
> One of the original motives for conceiving Fafhrd and the Mouser was to have a couple of fantasy heroes closer to true human stature than supermen like Conan and Tarzan and many another. In a way

they're a mixture of Cabell and Eddison, if we must look for literary ancestors. Fafhrd and the Mouser have a touch of Jurgen's cynicism and anti-romanticism, but they go on boldly having adventures—one more roll of the dice with destiny and death. While the characters they most parallel in *The Worm Ouroboros* are Corund and Gro, yet I don't think they're touched with evil as those two, rather they're rogues in a decadent world where you have to be a rogue to survive; perhaps, in legendry, Robin Hood comes closest to them, though they're certainly a pair of lone-wolf Robin Hoods....

They are the Robin Hood and Little John of the urban alleys, an Asterix and Obelix with adult temptations. Indeed, the attitude of Goscinny and Uderzo to incompetent wizards and pompous authorities is remarkably similar to Leiber's, only Leiber's satire extends to gods and symbols as well as wizards:

Sitting on his dark-cushioned, modest throne in his low, rambling castle in the heart of the Shadowland, Death shook his pale head and pommeled a little his opalescent temples and slightly pursed his lips, which were the color of violet grapes with the silvery bloom still on, above his slender figure armored in chain mail and his black belt, studded with silver skulls tarnished almost as black, from which hung his irresistible sword.

He was a relatively minor Death, only the Death of the World of Nehwon, but he had his problems. Tenscore flickering or flaring human lives to have their wicks pinched in the next twenty heartbeats. And although the heartbeats of Death resound like a leaden bell far underground and each has a little of eternity in it, yet they do finally pass. Only nineteen left now. And the Lords of Necessity, who outrank Death, still to be satisfied.

"The Sadness of the Executioner," 1973

87

There is a discipline to Leiber's prose which lifts it beyond comparison with any of his predecessors and were it not that Leiber himself was apparently too modest to produce a large fantastic novel, one from him would surely be the best of its kind. Perhaps that very scepticism which colours the Fafhrd and Gray Mouser stories is what has made him hesitate up to now. These are not the ecstatic, wish-fulfilment fantasies of passionate adolescence, nor are they mere fables of human folly. They are generous-hearted adventure fantasy for grown-ups as surely as Stevenson's later historical novels or Hammett's thrillers were for grown-ups. Popular fiction is sadly short of such talents.

L. Sprague De Camp and Fletcher Pratt, who also appeared in *Unknown* at the same time as Leiber, produced for a time an excellent series of spoof stories featuring Harold Shea, a rather bookish sceptic who was plunged into various fabulous or romantic worlds, usually against his will. De Camp in particular has a deep interest in history and has since written some exceptionally interesting historical novels set in the ancient world. He made it his business in various time-travel stories to debunk popular conceptions about the past. In an early story *Lest Darkness Fall* (1941) he sent his character—a descendant of Twain's Yankee—back to the late Roman Empire, and in many other stories he used this device to show his readers how people really might have lived and thought in the past. Shea had adventures in the worlds of *Kubla Khan*, *The Faerie Queene*, *Orlando Furioso*, and various other literary and mythical lands of the imagination. It is sad that most of De Camp's last work in this genre was as a collaborator in writing various pastiches of the Conan stories. I suspect he had a playful relish for bad writing and little judgement where it is concerned for in *Conan of the Isles* (1968), a collaboration with Lin Carter, we get passage after passage of this kind:

> "Sigurd of Vanaheim, you fat old walrus! By the scarlet bowels of Hell—Sigurd Redbeard! "he roared, rising to clasp the burly seaman in his arms.
>
> "Amra of the *Red Lion*!" cried Sigurd.
>
> "Hush; hold your tongue, you old banel of whale blubber!" growled Conan. "I've reason to remain

nameless for a while."

"Oh," said Sigurd. In a lower voice he continued: "By the breasts of Badb and the claws of Nergal, broil my guts if it don't warm an old seaman's heart to clap eyes on you!"

They hugged each other like angry bears, then drew apart to pummel each other on the shoulders with buffets that would have sent lesser men staggering.

"Sigurd, by Crom! Sit and drink with me, you barnacled old whale!" Conan roared. The other collapsed, wheezing on the bench across from the Cimmerian. He doffed his plumed hat and stretched fat legs with a gusty sigh.

"Taverner!" boomed Conan. "Another cup, and where's that cursed roast?"

"By Mitra's golden sword and Wodun's league-long spear, ye haven't changed a mite in thirty years!" said the red-bearded Vanir when they had toasted each other. He dragged one crimson cuff across bristling lips and emitted a mighty belch.

"Haven't I, you lying old rogue?" Conan chuckled. "Why, thirty years ago, when I hit a man in the face like that, I broke his jaw and sometimes his neck as well." He sighed. "But old man Time hunts us all down at the last. You've changed, too, Sigurd; that fat gut was as slim as a topsail yard when last we met. Remember how we were becalmed off the Nameless Isles, with naught to eat but the rats in the hold and what few stinking fish we could dredge out of Manannan's wet lair?"

"Aye, aye," the other chuckled, wiping sentimental tears from his eye. "Oh, damn me guts, of course ye've changed, old Lion!"

This is mindless, silly, heartless stuff which would disgrace even a schoolboy imitator of Conan, let alone one of science fiction's most careful writers. The work is almost certainly Carter's (being pretty typical) but De Camp surely owed it to the Howard he admired to ensure better editing, for Conan was never more dead than he is in these travesties of the original stories. More recently the original stories have been reissued in England and America and stand as a monument to Howard's popular vitality and fluency.

After his collaboration with Pratt in the '40s, De Camp went on to write a number of epic fantasies that were not spoofs or imitations. Chief of these is *The Tritonian Ring* which borrows certain traditional themes from Greek mythology and whose hero is Prince Vakar of Lorsk (a nation on the lost continent Poseidonis). What makes this book attractive is that, although De Camp is content to write about a conventional and slightly daft hero, his control over his material is such that we are always aware of the hero's defects while remaining sympathetic to him. We are introduced to him like this:

> On the king's left sat his younger son Vakar, the twin (but not the identical twin) brother of Kuros, looking a bit vacuous (for age and experience had not yet stamped his features with character) and a bit foppish.... Instead of the normal Pusadian kilt he wore the checkered trews of the barbarians, and (another fad) copied the barbarian custom of shaving all the face but the upper lip.

As well as a supernatural element, this romance has a picture of the world in transition from Bronze Age to Iron Age, and its hero, like Airar Alvarson, has changed somewhat between the book's beginning and its end.

Doubtless reflecting the sober society of the forties and fifties, which had perhaps seen enough of corrupted romanticism in the heraldry, rhetoric and ritual of Nazi Germany (see Norman Spinrad's spoof on the genre *The Iron Dream*, 1972) the heroes of this kind of fantasy were much more down-to-earth and practical fellows, like Jack Vance's Turjan of Miir in *The Dying Earth* (1950):

> ... Did the idiotic visage conceal perception, a will to extinction? As Turjan watched, the white-blue eyes closed, the great head slumped and bumped to the

floor of the cage. These limbs relaxed: the creature was dead.

Turjan sighed and left the room. He mounted winding stone stairs and at last came out on the roof of his castle Miir, high above the river Derna. In the west the sun hung close to old earth; ruby shafts, heavy and rich as wine, slanted past the gnarled holes of the archaic forest to lie on the turfed forest floor. The sun sank in accordance with the old ritual; latter-day night fell across the forest, a soft, warm darkness came swiftly, and Turjan stood pondering the death of his latest creature.

Vance's stories remind me of the delicate oriental fantasies of Frank Owen, a neglected *Weird Tales* writer who published a few collections of stories in the thirties, was reprinted in the fifties, but has not, to my knowledge, appeared since.

In 1954 Poul Anderson published what is for me the best story of its kind, *The Broken Sword,* which I reread recently for the review found in the appendices. The strong Scandinavian influence combined with a sophisticated view of Alfheim perhaps owing something to Spenser. His Elf-lords are both more attractive and more sympathetic than his human characters. Unlike most generic fantasy Anderson's story is a true tragedy. A human child is exchanged for a troll-born changeling. Scafloc the human is raised in Faerie, amongst the immortal, sardonic elves. He falls under the power of his own evil sword. Valgard the changeling becomes a bewildered, alienated berserker in the world of men, betraying and killing in his desperate quest for a world where he can feel at home. The tragedy begins to play itself out, inevitably. This superb tale is Anderson's finest dramatic achievement. His *Three Hearts and Three Lions*, also owing something to *A Connecticut Yankee in King Arthur's Court,* is set in the world of Charlemagnian Romance and again gives us a glimpse of the bitter-sweet world of Faerie. Both novels are published in the outstanding Fantasy Masterworks series edited by Jo Fletcher and Malcolm Edwards for Victor Gollancz.

Be wary of Anderson's later work which varies enormously in ambition and character. His first published novel was a detective story, his second was an authentic saga. *The Broken Sword* remains my favourite book in the genre and the one from which I derived considerable inspiration for my own early stories.

In my view John Brunner's fantasy, like Anderson's, contained some of his best writing and more resonances than his sf, perhaps because the sf has to rationalize and, to a degree at least, destroy the force of the original vision. Brunner's central character in four novellas is the Traveller in Black, a sardonic, mysterious figure who travels through a universe ruled by magic, battling the forces of Chaos. The book was published in the USA in 1971 as *The Traveller in Black* and has since been reprinted in the UK but it is time it had another reprint. Brunner's character was refreshingly unusual, appearing as he did at a time when there were few intelligent protagonists about.

Unfortunately what seems like the majority of imitators who came in recent years to fulfil the demands of publishers sensing a commercial market were attracted to what is presumably a compensatory fantasy of homicidal barbarians and grunting rapists. As a result they produced characters even more terrifyingly simple-minded than Conan himself. The appeal was never easy for me to understand, but I was given a clue some years ago when, as a guest of a fantasy convention, I appeared on a panel with a group of sword-and-sorcery writers who told the audience that the reason they wrote such fantasy was because they (and, they implied, the audience) felt inadequate to cope with the complexities of modern life. "Where today?" asked one, "can you put an arm hold around a man's throat and slip a knife into him between the third and fourth ribs and get away with it?" The answer was, of course, that the Marines were still looking for recruits. But maybe he meant, "Where can you do that and not have someone retaliate?" If that's the main appeal of such stories it probably explains why most people over the age of eighteen stop reading them.

One other less violently-disposed writer, whose characters were not mindless butchers, was Andre Norton. Although I find her protagonists somewhat too wholesome for my own taste, she has produced a great deal of good quality fantasy which has had a marked influence on the writers who came after her, particularly the women. Norton's sword-wielding riders of dragons and unicorns are young women. This doesn't make her fiction necessarily "feminist" and her use of women in what had traditionally been a male role is no more than simple reversal, but they offer a more palatable alternative to Cronk the Berserker. Largely designed to be read about by young adults, her heroines are filled with a love of nature and display a caring sentimentality towards the world at large. Better, surely, to suffer that than to be subjected to characters who have the political sophistication of a storm trooper and the sensitivity of a bad-tempered wolverine. Norton's influence has perhaps been unfortunate, in that sometimes one begins to think the only alternative to Brute is Cute, and one grows sick, these days, of a surfeit of healers, unicorns, nurturers and beast-tamers. One begins to long to come across a female protagonist called, say, Naomi the Castrator. One could tell her to look up John Norman, for a start (but more of that later...).

Cute has by no means become the province of women fantasts. Many men, presumably also sickened by the plethora of barbarians, have produced extremely sentimental work. Violence, after all, is only the other side of the sentimental coin, as the behaviour of, for instance, concentration camp commandants frequently testifies.

Another slightly off-beat hero is Stephen Donaldson's Thomas Covenant, leper and minor amputee, who wakes up after a car accident to find himself in a world known as The Land, dominated by evil Lord Foul. In some ways Covenant resembles a character in one of Ron Hubbard's *Unknown* stories (*Slaves of Sleep* or *Typewriter in the Sky*) in that he frequently wonders at his entrapment in a world whose reality is by no means certain. Through six long books (which owe rather more to Tolkien than I find tolerable) Covenant pursues his adventures, though a second, female, protagonist (Linden Avery) adds a certain amount of interest to the final three volumes (which are also, I think, an improvement on the first three):

> "No." Her contradiction cut him off, though she did
> not shout. She had become too clenched and furious
> for shouting, too extreme to be denied. "He's not
> you. He's not the one who's going to die." She might
> have said, I'm the one who kills —The words were
> plain in every line of her visage. But her passion

carried her past that recognition as if she could not bear it in any other way. "Everybody makes mistakes. But all you've done is try to fight for what you love. You have an answer. I don't." The heat of her assertion contained no self-pity. "I haven't had one since this thing started. I don't know the Land the way you do. I haven't got any power. All I've been able to do is follow you around." Her hands rose into fists. "If you're going to die, do something to make it count!"

Then like a quick touch of ice he realized that she had not come here to question him simply because the First desired a destination. *She wants to know where we're going.* Her father had killed himself and blamed her for it; and she had killed her mother with her own hands; and now his, Covenant's, death seemed as certain as the Desecration of the Earth. But those things served only to give her the purpose he had lost. She was wearing her old severity now— the same rigid self-punishment and determination with which she had defied him from the moment of their first meeting. It was the unanswered anger of her grief, and it swept all costs aside in its desire for battle.

White Gold Wielder, 1983

At least Donaldson's characters are adults and are attempting to deal with adult (albeit exaggerated) concerns. The infantile element in epic fantasy still tends to dominate the vast number of books presently being published. This element is perhaps most markedly evident in the work of a writer who originally began a series of books specifically commissioned by Messrs. Ballantine to be directly in the tradition of Edgar Rice Burroughs. The early stories of Tarl Cabot, starting with *Tarnsman of Gor*, by John Norman were fairly competent (if somewhat dull) imitations of the Martian books. Soon, however, they became increasingly—now almost wholly—obsessed with a crude form of sado-masochism which, while it is as far removed from *The Story of O* as *I, The Jury* is from *The Lady in the Lake*, was quite as pernicious.

Marked by a droning, obsessive tone, common to much neurotic fantasy, the current Gor books go further than any other books of their kind toward reflecting the aggressive terror of adulthood, sexuality and women in particular, common to so many of them.

Tarl Cabot, who began life as a descendant of John Carter, who was himself a descendant of Allan Quatermain, has a relish for sham and wanton cruelty far more ludicrous, in context, than Quatermain's somewhat pompous chivalry (though both, again, can be seen as sides of the same coin):

> Whereas fear inhibits sexual performance in a male, rendering it impossible, because neutralizing aggression, essential to male power, fear in a woman, some fear, not terror, can, interestingly, improve her responsiveness, perhaps by facilitating her abject submission, which can then lead to multiple orgasms. This is another reason, incidentally, why Goreans favor the enslavement of desirable women; the slave girl knows that she must please her master, and that she will be punished, and perhaps harshly, if she does not; this makes her not only desperate to please the brute who fondles her, but also produces in her a genuine fear of him; this fear on her part enhances her receptivity and responsiveness; also, of course, since fear stimulates aggression, which is intimately connected with male sexuality, her fear, which she is unable to help, to her master's amusement, deepens and augments the very predation in which she finds herself as quarry; and if she should not be afraid, it is no great matter; any woman, if the master wishes, can be taught fear.
>
> *Marauders of Gor*, Book 9 of the series, 1975

Although laughably out of place in an epic fantasy tale this stuff is read primarily by adolescent boys who might be as frightened sexually as the author seems to be. They must frequently feel they are learning what real life is all about. As the blood-and-thunder hacks pretend they are writing of the harsh facts of life and death, so do pornographers pretend they are writing realistically about sex, dignifying themselves as being victimized for telling the truth. I find such writers feeble-minded at best.

At worst they are frighteningly dangerous—for this is, like much present-day fiction, so unimaginative, so seedy in its brutal attitudes towards human beings (especially women), so aggressively sterile, so hypocritical and ambiguous in its moral and social values, that one can only mourn for the tree which was cut down to make the paper on which it was printed.

It is a relief to mention an excellent writer, one of the newer generation, Robin McKinley, whose central character Angharad ("Harry") Crewe is a personable young woman able to bring just the right note of perfect credibility to a tale of wonder:

> Then she found that she remembered her parents together again; as if her mother had died recently, or her father five years ago—or as if the difference, which had seemed so important, no longer mattered. She didn't dream of honeysuckle and lilac. She remembered them with affection, but she looked across the swirled sand and small obstinate clumps of brush and was content with where she was. A small voice whispered to her that she didn't even want to go Home again. She wanted to cross the desert and climb into the mountains in the east, the mountains no Homelander had ever climbed.
> *The Blue Sword*, 1982

McKinley is representative of the best of the modern fantasts. There is nothing cute or apologetic about her characters, neither are they brutal, mindless or cruel. This is true of many others, including Patricia McKillip:

> She unlocked the gates, her fingers shaking in an anger that roused through her like a clean mountain wind. She snapped private calls into the dream-drugged minds about her, and, like pieces of dreams

themselves, the animals moved toward her.
The Forgotten Beasts of Eld, 1980

With the exception of Wolfe and Harrison, most of the interesting fantasy at present seems to be coming from women. Mary Gentle, Storm Constantine, Joan Vinge, Lisa Goldstein, Elizabeth A. Lynn, Katherine Kurtz and lately K. J. Bishop have all done good and original work. Since the epic fantasy form has always tended to put rather more accent on personalities and relationships than, say, science fiction, it's an ideal form for good women writers to turn to their own uses. The form is likely to reach its finest flowering in the hands of aggressive, defiantly independent women but I would still like to see a few more fantasies like Joanna Russ's *The Female Man* (1975), making genuinely original use of the genre. There's still a disappointing amount of simple role reversal, of strong, paternal background figures "helping" the heroine in her adventures, of leggy teenagers getting enthusiastic about being allowed to ride a lot of horses. A past generation was subject to one of the great cross-influences which brought us a number of women writers choosing to write fantasy rather than write the historical romance popularised by Jean Plaidy, Norah Lofts and, on a somewhat different plane, Mary Renault. These writers seem to have spawned more than a few imitators who, rather than do the historical research, have chosen to set their timeless love-stories in fairytale lands even further divorced from reality than the worlds of Georgette Heyer and Baroness Orczy. These are by no means, I suppose, as irritating as the male equivalent (i.e. John Norman), but they are almost as bad in some ways because they so often present conventional stereotypical images of male and female relationships, continuing to show men as "masterful" and women as fundamentally passive. Rambofiction makes much the same statements. Whether their authors realize it or not, they are involved in mass-production. Instead of carving their dolls at a factory bench, they are doing piece-work at home.

While it is very easy to grow tired of the chatty or intimate style in which a lot of generic fantasy is now written it is sometimes almost impossible to get to grips with the excessively distanced narratives typical of Morris or Dunsany. Sometimes such a writer will give that kind of narrative greater dimension by the use of the first person, but more often they will will merge their characters so thoroughly into the landscape that they will cease to be heroes, in any real sense, at all. Something of this tendency could be found in M. John Harrison's early fantasy, carving its own path to glory.

While he had a relish for his characters, they were sometimes described in entirely visual terms, which gave us difficulty in sensing them as individuals. Also he was inclined to prefer groups of heroes, as Eddison sometimes did, rather than a single central character, so that in *The Pastel City* (1971) we have a selection of heroes but no real protagonist. The nearest thing to a hero is introduced in Chapter One:

> tegeus-Cromis, sometime soldier and sophisticate of Viriconium, the Pastel City, who now dwelt quite alone in a tower by the sea and imagined himself a better poet than a swordsman, stood at early morning on the sand-dunes that lay between his tall home and the grey line of the surf. Like swift and tattered scraps of rag, black gulls sped and fought over his downcast head. It was a catastrophe that had driven him from his tower, something that he had witnessed from its topmost room during the night.

This tendency is one Harrison shares with the late Thomas Burnett Swann, who began publishing in the fifties with stories set in the fabulous ancient world where Greek and Roman deities still flourished, though their time was almost done. Writing in the first person Swann sustained his narrative adequately:

> Where is the bird of fire? In the tall green flame of the cypress, I see his shadow, flickering with the swallows. In the city that crowds the Palatine, where Fauns walk with men and wolves are fed in the temples, I hear the rush of his wings. But that is his shadow and sound. The bird himself is gone. Always his wings beat just beyond my hands, and the wind possesses his cry. Where is the bird of fire? Look up,

he burns in the sky, with Saturn and the Golden Age.
I will go to find him.
"Where is the Bird of Fire?," 1970

Usually Swann's heroes are pre-pubescent or adolescent boys and girls. Here is the opening of "Vashti ," reprinted in the same volume as the title story above:

> His mind and memories were those of a young man, but his face and body belonged to a child of six. He was small and smooth and as bright as the sunbirds which clicker like will-o-the wisps through the forests of the Black Continent. His eyes were the green of young acorns, his lips were the red of poppy buds, and his hair seemed woven of honey strained from a comb and spun into supple strands. Noble ladies liked to caress and fondle him and feed him sugared dates, but when he began to recite the songs of Sappho or the theorems of Pythagoras, they dropped their hands and muttered incantations as if he were an evil-working Jinn. His name was Ianiskos, the "Little Healer." At least, that was the name which the Greeks had given him before he came to Persia to serve in the court of Xerxes, the king.

Swann, for all his predilections, could still draw primitives who were neither naïve nor emotionally coarse and in this he shares something with the greatest and most neglected of historical novelists Henry Treece, whose novels of Celtic Britain are the finest I have ever read. There could be a whole book on Arthurian fiction which would include Malory, Tennyson, Swinburne, Morris, Twain, Pyle, Steinbeck and White, and might extend, perhaps, into Celtic historical fiction in general. I would guess that Frazer's *Golden Bough* is a fairly recent central influence. Of all the talented exponents of this sort of fiction—Sutcliffe, Garner, Cooper—Treece is the best. *The Golden Strangers*, *The Dark Island* and *The Great Captains* (about Arthur) are models of their kind and superior to Treece's later work (*Red Queen*, *White Queen*; *Electra*; *The Green Man;* etc.) which have been more often reprinted. Treece's savages and barbarians are neither noble nor brutish, childish nor sadistic, but living individuals, interpreting their world in mystical and sometimes cruel terms. There are no true supernatural elements in Treece's books, but there is a greater sense of the supernatural than in almost all epic fantasy ever written. To his heroes the landscapes that surround them are full of significance, of hope and terror. Most recently published by the defiant, original and idealistic Savoy Books, and still available from their website.

Keith Roberts, author of Pavane, an alternate world fantasy of considerable power, and *The Boat of Fate*, an impressive historical novel, has written a good deal in this *Golden Bough* vein and his introspective barbarian heroes are often the equal of Treece's. Here is a passage from *The Chalk Giants* (1974), a book which appeared in the USA in a badly mutilated edition:

> He flexed his hands, stammering in his eagerness. "This was my dream," he said. "That I was the grain, and earth, and creeping things upon it. And mist and sky, the stones the Giants placed between the hills. I was the land, Miri, and the land was me. In the dream I found a woman, who was also the land; and we made children who would…now the land, and live out golden times. And…this too was the dream. That we died, returning to earth; but we were our children, and their children's children, and the golden grain again. It seemed a…mystery, a worthy thing."

This is a world after a great disaster, where men repeat their myths and their history according to archetypal, unconscious urgings and tell tales of the past:

> "In the old times," it said, "the Giants came. Elwin Mydroylin was King in the West. The warboats came, the boats of floating iron. Forests grew on their decks. Others sailed beneath the water, hurling javelins that scorched the earth. The crops were withered, and trees in the passes next the sea. The cities of the Giants

were destroyed. Elwin Mydroylin went down to night, and his sons who killed the Dragon on Brondin Mere. He saw the love of women, and it was false. He saw the love of men, and it was false. The Dragons came in the north. The hills were shaken."

Compare this to the flaccid sentimentalism of most of the current crop of "Celtic" writers, the halting simplification of language which lacks all the strength of that which it seeks to imitate, like Evangeline Walton's re-telling of the Mabinogion:

> He woke suddenly, as if a bell had been rung in his ear. Startled, he peered round him, but saw only sight-swallowing blackness that soon thinned to a darkness full of things yet darker. Of half-shaped, constantly reshaping somethings such as always haunt the lightless depths of night, and make it seem mysterious and terrible. He saw nothing that meant anything, and if he had heard anything he did not hear it again.
>
> Then, sharp as an order, came memory: *"You have come to hunt in Glen Cuch, so why not get to it?"*
>
> "By the God my people swear by, I will do that!" said Pwyll and he jumped out of bed.
> *Prince of Annwyn*, 1974

Books of this kind have heroes as limp as their prose, but seem astonishingly to pass for literature amongs a certain semi-academic readership. There is a small industry in them, these days. It is written by people busily turning it into a genre as far removed from its roots as the average Gothic romance or love-story is removed from *Jane Eyre*. It is romanticism corrupted to sentimentalism. Finn Mac Coul takes tea in middle-class drawing rooms and has the refined sensitivity of a Victorian curate; the landscapes of wild, old Ireland become the well-kept back-gardens of the suburbs.

Macpherson has a lot to answer for.

Happily, there are still writers who can evoke a sense of ancient Britain in their work. Gillian Bradshaw's hero, what's more, begins life as a pretty poor specimen:

When my father received the news of the Pendragon's death, I was playing boats by the sea.

I was then eleven years old, and as poor a warrior as any boy in my father's realm of the Innsi Erc, the Orcades Islands. Since I also was a very poor hunter, I had little in common with the other boys, the sons of the noble clans of our island, with whom I lived and trained in the Boys' House, and I had still less in common with my elder brother, Agravain, who led the others in making my life difficult; almost as difficult as my father's plans for me did. To escape from the insistent world of warriors and warriors-to-be, I went sometimes to my younger brother, but more often to a secret place I had by the sea.
Hawk of May, 1981

While here is Holdstock:

And at that moment I realised that the piping had stopped, and Guiwenneth too had stopped, a few paces away from me. She stared around her, at the flickering lights in the darkness. A moment later she looked back at me, her face pale, her eyes wide, her mouth open; from being delighted, she suddenly was terrified. She took a step towards me, my name on her lips, and I was caught in her sudden panic, and reached for her....

There was a strange sound, like wind, like a hoarse, tuneless whistle, and then the sound of a thump and Keeton's gasping cry. I glanced at him and he was stepping rapidly backwards, arched back, clutching at his chest, his eyes screwed tight shut with pain. A moment later he fell to the ground, arms outstretched. Three feet of wood shaft jutted from his body. "Guin!" I screamed, tearing my gaze from Keeton. And then all around us the woodland burst into brilliant fire, the trunks catching, the branches, the leaves, so that the garden was surrounded by a great, roaring wall of flame. Two dark human shapes came bursting through that fire, light glinting on metal armour and the short-bladed weapons held in their hands. For a moment they hesitated, staring at us; one had the golden mask of a hawk, its eyes mere slits, the ears rising like short horns from the crown. The other wore a dull leather helmet, the cheek straps broad. The hawk laughed loudly.

"Oh God no…! " I cried, but Guiwenneth screamed at me, "Arm yourself!" as she raced past me to where her own weapons were lodged against the back wall of the house.

Mythago Wood, 1984

One should also mention both Mary Stewart and Rosemary Sutcliff as important influences on much modern fantasy. Both writers have produced excellent cycles of stories based on the Arthurian myth. Here is a taste of Stewart:

Not every king would care to start his reign with the wholesale massacre of children. This is what they whisper of Arthur, even though in other ways he is held up as the type itself of the noble ruler, the protector alike of high and lowly.

The Last Enchantment, 1979

And here is Sutcliff:

Then Arthur took the sword two-handed by its quillions. There was golden writing on the stone, but he did not stop to read it. The sword seemed to thrill under his touch as a harp thrills in response to its master's hand. He felt strange, as though he were on the point of learning some truth that he had forgotten before he was born. The thin winter sunlight was so piercing-bright that he seemed to hear it; a high white music in his blood.

The Sword and the Circle, 1981

Gene Wolfe, whose models seem to go no further back in time than two or three hundred years, has produced one of the most original central characters to appear in epic fantasy. Wolfe's narrator Severian, the Torturer, looks at the world through genuinely unconventional eyes, although he is very much a creature of his own world. His ideas of right and wrong, of good conduct, of decent style and taste are frequently not at all close to our own. His discursive, lively style most frequently resembles Gulliver's or some other early 18th century adventurer and Wolfe, through him, keeps us interested whether it be on the subject of hybrid dog-wolves, fairytales of the far future, the true nature of magic, the morality of friendship, the qualities of a beast which for a short while absorbs the idiosyncrasies of whomever it eats, so that it can speak for a while like its victim and continue to express the desires of that victim. By introducing archaicisms into his story, casually and rarely explained, Wolfe adds to the sense of reality of his account. I think another reason why Wolfe's narrative is superior to most is because he cares more for his people and therefore automatically impresses us with an urgent desire for their well-being, for knowledge of their affairs. Stories sustain themselves best when they have such people in them. Wolfe's Grand Master of the Orders of the Seekers for Truth and Penitence, Severian, is also that rare creature in fantasy, an unreliable narrator. You can never be absolutely sure that he is telling you the truth. He is also never backward in offering his opinions.

> I have never encountered men whose language, costume, or customs are foreign without speculating on the nature of the women of their race. There is always a connection, since the two are the growths of a single culture, just as the leaves of a tree, which one sees, and the fruit, which one does not see because it is hidden by the leaves, are the growths of a single organism. But the observer who would venture to predict the appearance and the flavour of the fruit from the outline of a few leafy boughs seen (as it were) from a distance, must know a great deal about leaves and fruit if he is not to make himself

ridiculous.

Warlike men may be born of languishing women, or they may have sisters nearly as strong as themselves and more resolute. And so I, walking among crowds, composed largely of these eclectics and the townsmen (who seemed to me not much different from the citizens of Nessus, save that their clothing and their manners were somewhat rougher) found myself speculating on dark-eyed dark-skinned women, women with glossy black hair as thick as the tails of the skewbald mounts of their brothers, women whose faces I imagined as strong yet delicate, women given to ferocious resistance and swift surrender, women who could be won but not bought—if such women exist in this world.

From their arms I travelled in imagination to the places where they might be found, the lonely huts crouched by mountain springs, the hide yurts standing along in the high pastures. Soon I was as intoxicated with thought of the mountains as I had been once, before Master Paleamon had told me the correct location of Thrax, with the idea of the sea.

The Sword of the Lictor, 1982

All in all, the Gene Wolfe books possess a style, imagination and intelligence which is rare enough in contemporary epic fantasy. Like Harrison's, his is a talent which, I would guess, would excel in whatever form it chose.

Harrison's most recent fantasy stories have given us a selection of characters all of whom are more clearly described and observed than earlier ones. They tend towards grotesque extraversion (which Harrison in a quintessential English way seems to equate with villainy or moral weakness) or brooding introspection. If Wolfe's Severian is a mixture of Manchu mandarin, Roman senator and 18th century *picaro*, then Harrison's characters seem to emerge more from a late 19th century *fin-de-siècle* ambience, as, for instance, with Ardwick Crome:

Every morning he would write for perhaps two hours, first restricting himself to the bed by means of three broad leather straps which his father had given him and which he fastened himself, at the ankles, the hips, and finally across his chest. The sense of unfair confinement or punishment induced by this, he found, helped him to think.

"The Luck in the Head," *Viriconium Nights*, 1985

Some come from perhaps a slightly earlier romantic period. This description, of the chief protagonist, might equally have suited Swinburne:

He was a strange little man to have got the sort of reputation he had. At first sight his clients, who often described themselves later as victims, thought little of him. His wedge-shaped head was topped by a coxcomb of red hair which gave him a permanently shocked expression. His face accentuated this, being pale and bland of feature, except the eyes which were very large and wide. He wore the ordinary clothes of the time, and one steel ring he had been told was valuable. He had few close friends in the city. He came from a family of rural landlords somewhere in the midlands; no-one knew them. (This accident of birth had left him a small income: and entitled him to wear a sword, although he never bothered. He had one somewhere in a cupboard.)

In Viriconium, 1982

This is Ashlyme, the artist, whose attempts to communicate with and rescue another painter, Audsley King, constitute the main thread of narrative. There is a mysterious plague upon Viriconium. While many choose to ignore its existence, Ashlyme becomes obsessed with it. Meanwhile, strange, careless gods manifest themselves in Viriconium and new lords appear as rulers of the city, as eccentric and hard to place as Viriconium herself.

Harrison, whose own early enthusiasms encompassed a great deal of traditional English fantasy, has come a long way from his sources. While the trappings and exotic appeal of the epic fantasy are retained, he has made of the form something altogether idiosyncratic. Harrison's heroes and heroines are, though frequently attractive and sympathetic, almost the same as earlier villains. Scott, with his robust sense of what a gentleman should be, would see only Oriental decadence here. And Harrison has come almost as far as possible from, say, *Amadis of Gaul*. As John J . O'Connor remarks in his excellent *Amadis de Gaule and its influence on Elizabethan Literature* (1970), "The life of a knight in *Amadis de Gaule* is, above all, a life of action, and his virtue is almost always muscular...Since the only way for a knight to achieve virtue and glory in this life is through combat, the twenty-one books of *Amadis* are saturated with fights. In Book VII, for example, there are more than forty of them, and this number does not include encounters with lions, bears, or other nonhuman opponents."

In keeping with Harrison's characteristic challenging of every genre convention, there are battles in Viriconium but they are usually off-stage. If there are fights, they are as a rule seedy brawls in which everyone is hurt and nothing is resolved, while Ashlyme's nonhuman opponents adopt the guise of guffawing hooligans whose chief acts involve the scattering of garbage in the streets at night, and who are puzzled by the idea of anyone wanting to attack them. In the new books the magical and epic elements are combined with characters who have genuine passions, adult concerns, complex motives. It seems that in the best of these we shall soon no longer be able to discover heroes or heroines but read instead about real people. It will be interesting to see if the form will be able to take the strain!

4
WIT AND HUMOUR

Farther, I remember marking the flowers in the frame
of carved oak, and casting my eye on the pistols which
hang beneath, being the fire-arms with which, in the
eventful year of 1746, my uncle meant to have
espoused the cause of Prince Charles Edward; for,
indeed, so little did he esteem personal safety, in
comparison of steady high-church principle, that he
waited but the news of the Adventurer's reaching
London to hasten to join his standard.
Sir Walter Scott, Introduction, *Peveril of the Peak*,
1820

Scott's wit redeemed his work and makes it possible for us to
enjoy it today in spite of its long-windedness, its unlikely plots,
its unfashionable sentiment. His humorous characters relieve
the sober heart-searchings of his main characters. Scott, inheriting
the style of the great 18th century novelists, could hardly fail to
supply that wit, though he frequently spread it as thinly as he spread
the rest of his talents.

Fantastic fiction is happily very rich in comedy, from Thomas
Love Peacock to Mervyn Peake. Comedy demands paradox, the
juxtaposition of disparate images and elements, just as fantasy does.
The square peg was never more delightful than when trying to fit
itself into the round hole of a De Camp and Pratt fantasy. Comedy,
like fantasy, is often at its best when making the greatest possible
exaggerations whereas tragedy usually becomes bathetic when it

exaggerates. Obviously there is a vast difference between, say, Lewis Carroll and Richard Garnett but the thing that all writers of comedy have in common is a fascination with grotesque and unlikely juxtapositions of images, characters and events: the core of most humour, from Hal Roach to Nabokov. Somehow, too, the attraction to wholehearted mythological subject matter is often coupled to a comic talent as in the work of Mark Twain and James Branch Cabell. With *A Connecticut Yankee in King Arthur's Court*, Twain produced one of the greatest classics of its kind, which has influenced more than one generation of fantasy writers. What gives Twain's romance a power which its imitators have in the main lacked is the undercurrent of pathos and tragedy running through the whole story. It is a substantial and enduring book because, although it is funny, it does not deny the facts and implications of its subject matter. The death of England's chivalry before The Boss's electric fences and gatlings is all the more poignant for the comedy which precedes the scene.

Jokes are not Comedy and stories which contain jokes are not comic stories. The art of ironic comedy is the highest art of all in fiction and drama but it is by no means the most popular art. James Branch Cabell's success with *Jurgen* (1919) was based on the public's mistaken idea that the book was filthy. It introduced enough people to Cabell's work, however, to give him a reasonably large audience through his lifetime. His books today are rarely reprinted, as Peacock's are rarely reprinted, perhaps because they are an acquired taste (like some Meredith novels) and no publisher seems prepared to publish sufficient of them to help anyone acquire that taste. A vicious circle. Here is an example of Cabell:

> Thus it was that, upon the back of the elderly and quite tame dragon, Miramon returned to his earlier pursuits and to the practice of what he—in his striking way of putting things,—described as art for art's sake. The episode of Manuel had been, in the lower field of merely utilitarian art, amusing enough. That stupid, tall, quiet posturer, when he set out to redeem Poictesme, had needed just the mere bit of elementary magic which Miramon had performed for him, to establish Manuel among the great ones of the earth.

Miramon had, in consequence, sent a few obsolete gods to drive the Northmen out of Poictesme, while Manuel waited upon the sands north of Manneville and diverted his leisure by contemplatively spitting into the sea. Thereafter Manuel had held the land to the admiration of everybody but more particularly of Miramon,—who did not at all agree with Anavalt of Fomor in his estimation of Dom Manuel's mental gifts.

The Silver Stallion, 1926

It seems always to have been true that the more grandiose, the more portentous, the less concise, the less truthful, the more humourless a writer is, the more successful he is; at least in his lifetime.

I think my own dislike of J. R. R. Tolkien lies primarily in the fact that in all those hundreds of pages, full of high ideals, sinister evil and noble deeds, there is scarcely a hint of irony anywhere. Its tone is one of relentless nursery room sobriety: "Once upon a time," began nanny gravely, for the telling of stories was a serious matter, "there were a lot of furry little people who lived happily in the most beautiful, gentlest countryside you could possibly imagine, and then one day they learned that Wicked Outsiders were threatening this peace...."

There are, of course, some whimsical jokes in Tolkien, some universal ironies, but these only serve to exaggerate the paucity of genuine imaginative invention. The jokes are not there to point to the truth, but to reject it. The collapse down the centuries of the great myths into whimsical nursery tales is mirrored in recent fiction: we have gone from hobbits, to seagulls, to rabbits and a whole host of other assorted talking vermin in a few short years and reached the ridiculous stage where there is often more substance to the children's books of writers like Garner, Garfield, Le Guin, Aitken and Cooper than there is in those fantasies apparently produced for adults! That such nostalgic pre-pubescent yearnings should find a large audience in England is bad enough, but that they should have international appeal is positively terrifying.

There is a specific method employed by bad writers to avoid the implications of their subject matter, to reduce the tensions, to minimize the importance of themes which they might, in pretending to write a serious book, inadvertently touch upon. This is the joke which specifically indicates to the reader that the story is not really "true." I'm reminded of my favourite line from Robert Heinlein's *Farnham's Freehold* where the daughter of the family, undergoing painful and primitive childbirth, pauses in her efforts to speak to her father. "Sorry about the sound-effects, daddy," she remarks with stoic cheer.

The laboured irony, as it were, of the pulp hero or heroine, this deadly levity in the face of genuine experience, which serves not to point up the dramatic effect of the narrative, but to reduce it, to make the experience described comfortingly unreal, is the trick of the worst kind of escapist author who pretends to be writing about fundamental truths and is in fact telling fundamental lies. An author of this kind cannot bear to confront reality for a second and will find any means of ignoring facts. Such wounded souls would be joking about the weather in Florida while they burned in Hell.

The great gaudy war-horses of heroic fantasy may look very fine in their silks, their cloth-of-gold, their silver, their iron, their richly decorated leather; they may roll their eyes and flare their nostrils and their huge hooves may dance proudly, but they are inclined to shy at the first hint of cannon-fire, to run, clanking and creaking, at the whistle of shot, to whinny in terror at the sight of blood, and return to the safety of their high-fenced field to make somewhat nervous jokes about the real issues not being decided in the mud and filth of the battle—but on some higher, cosmic plane.

What genuine humour can do, as in the work of Tolkien's contemporary, Mervyn Peake, is to emphasize the implications of its subject matter, to humanize its characters, clarify its issues and intensify its narrative. Humour is intrinsic to the *Gormenghast* trilogy (1945-59). Sonorous though much of the writing is, it is constantly saved from bathos by its wit, its shifts into dark comedy; melodramatic though many of the scenes can be, they are off-set by visual ironies, by comic juxtaposition, by sardonic descriptions, as with the Bright Carvers and their annual offerings (something BBC radio failed to understand when it produced its 1985 version). The injustices existing in Peake's world are injustices familiar to us all—cynicism; unfeeling self-involvement on the part of the powerful; confusion and fear on the part of the weak; unthinking brutality and inequalities, frustration and misery—yet these things are never harped upon; more often than not they are laughed at while the author bides his time.

There are genuine comic grotesques in Peake—the Prunesquallors, the Teachers, Swelter, Barquentine, the sisters Cora and Clarice—the Earl and the Countess of Groan themselves. Even the central character of the first two novels, the infamous Steerpike, is made to behave somewhat ridiculously on occasions, and when he takes his revenge on innocence—on those at whom we have laughed in earlier chapters—their plight is all the harder to endure; the pathos and misery of their situation is amplified and we see their fate in an altogether changed light. This is what the genuine comic writer can do, time after time. He or she can make us laugh only to pause with shock at the recognition of what we are actually laughing at: misery, despair, loneliness, humiliation, the fact of death.

Here is a short passage from the underrated third volume, *Titus Alone* (1959), where Titus has been arrested and is being tried for vagrancy:

> The Magistrate leaned forward on his elbows and rested his long, bony chin upon the knuckles of his interlocked fingers. "This is the fourth time that I have had you before me at the bar, and as far as I can judge, the whole thing has been a waste of time to the Court and nothing but a nuisance to myself. Your answers, when they have been forthcoming, have been either idiotic, nebulous, or fantastic. This cannot be allowed to go on. Your youth is no excuse. Do you like stamps?"
>
> "Stamps, your Worship?"
>
> "Do you collect them?"
>
> "No."
>
> "A pity. I have a rare collection rotting daily. Now listen to me. You have already spent a week in prison—but it is not your vagrancy that troubles me. That is straightforward, though culpable. It is that you are rootless and obtuse. It seems you have some knowledge hidden from us. Your ways are curious,

your terms are meaningless. I will ask you once again. What is this Gormenghast? What does it mean?"

Titus turned his face to the Bench. If ever there was a man to be trusted, his Worship was that man.

Ancient, wrinkled, like a tortoise, but with eyes as candid as grey glass.

But Titus made no answer, only brushing his forehead with the sleeve of his coat.

"Have you heard his Worship's question?" said a voice at his side. It was Mr. Drugg.

"I do not know," said Titus, "what is meant by such a question. You might just as well ask me what is this hand of mine? What does it mean?" And he raised it in the air with the fingers spread out like a starfish. "Or what is this leg?" And he stood on one foot in the box and shook the other as though it were loose. "Forgive me, your Worship, I cannot understand."

"It is a place, your Worship," said the Clerk of the Court. "The prisoner has insisted that it is a place."

"Yes, yes," said the Magistrate. "But where is it? Is it north, south, east, or west, young man? Help me to help you. I take it you do not want to spend the rest of your life sleeping on the roofs of foreign towns. What is it boy? What is the matter with you?"

A ray of light slid through a high window of the Courtroom and hit the back of Mr. Drugg's short neck as though it were revealing something of mystical significance. Mr. Drugg drew back his head and the light moved forward and settled on his ear. Titus watched it as he spoke.

"I would tell you, if I could, sir," he said. "I only know that I have lost my way. It is not that I want to return to my home—I do not; it is that even if I wished to do so I could not. It is not that I have travelled very far; it is that I have lost my bearings, sir."

"Did you run away, young man?"

"I rode away," said Titus.

"From…Gormenghast?"

"Yes, your Worship."

"Leaving your mother…?"

"Yes."

"And your father…?"

"No, not my father…"

"Ah...is he dead, my boy?"

"Yes, your Worship. He was eaten by owls."

The Magistrate raised an eyebrow and began to write upon a piece of paper.

Of all modern fantasts Mervyn Peake was probably the most successful at combining the comic with the epic to produce a trilogy which can be read and re-read for its insights into our own lives, showing our hopes and fears in a light which is often outrageously funny. The trilogy is reminiscent of Meredith's *The Amazing Marriage* (1896) for the skill with which epic, comic, tragic and moral elements are blended together. It stands above all other works of its type; the *Gormenghast* trilogy is the apotheosis of that romantic form which had its crude beginnings with *Castle of Otranto*, in which the vast, rambling, semi-ruined castle is a symbol of the mind itself.

"The optimist proclaims that we live in the best of all possible worlds," says Cabell, "and the pessimist fears that this is so." The optimist and the pessimist constantly war within writers of fiction as they give shape to their chosen subject matter. But it should be the subject matter, not the author's wishes, which ultimately speaks for itself. If an author forces the material one way or another to achieve a happy or an unhappy ending and thus denies the implications of what they have written they are betraying both the reader and themselves.

While I admire the ambition of James Branch Cabell ultimately I find his ironies too relentless. He cheats in order to show everything as an example of mere folly. In contrast to Twain, he uses his talents almost always to avoid pain, though he uses them very cleverly. Nothing is important, says Cabell, therefore nothing hurts. One becomes weary, after a while, of dismissive aphorisms. Like Vonnegut, he seems primarily concerned with showing how ridiculous all human activity can be; how pointless is human sorrow; how silly is human ambition; how pathetic is human concern and sentiment. It is anxiety-quelling of a sort which pretends to realism. It tells us that nothing is really worth suffering for to the extent that people are prepared to suffer; and that we debase ourselves by means of our self-deceits, our ridiculous vanities. But in the end this view is as untrue to our experience of life as that of the ponderous writer who insists that all issues are Large Issues, and that all Quests are in the end Rewarded if He Who Makes The Journey is Noble and Virtuous and given to inappropriate sentimentality. Cabell's kind of fiction may well act as a fine antidote to Tolkien's, but neither in the long run is very satisfying to the demanding reader.

The impulse to write dismissive ironies often emerges in reaction to an overdose of portentous and meretricious sobriety; but one, though pleasanter to read and considerably more palatable to digest, is finally no more enduring than the other.

Melodrama and irony work very well together; the best fantasies contain both elements, which maintain tonal equilibrium, but a work of fantasy must, to be outstanding, be something more than aesthetically pleasing, though God knows I suppose we should be grateful for the little that is merely that. Ideally it should have at its source some fundamental compassion for human beings, some ambition to show, by means of image, metaphor, elements of allegory, what human life is actually about. As with listening to the music of Mozart, of Ives or Schoenberg, we wish to be entertained, to escape the immediate pressures of the world—but we also wish, when we read, to be informed, to try to understand how we may deal with these problems and how we may respond positively, without cynicism, to the injustices and frustrations which constantly hamper the needs of the spirit.

Comedy and fantasy are close companions. If fantasy is real life exaggerated, more colourful and, perhaps, simpler; if the extremes of life are represented by giants and fairies, dragons and heroes, then the vicissitudes of life are represented, in farce at least, by a pratfall or a custard pie, an embarrassing misunderstanding, and the losing of one's trousers at a formal function. To offset the grandiose, the pompous elements in fantasy, the writer, like Fritz Leiber, will introduce comedy to add a dimension or two to the characters and thus involve the reader more thoroughly in concern for their fate. The degree of irony one employs can often determine the degree of sentiment one uses and if one does want to touch on matters about which one feels deeply, then it is often better to use a comic context.

Even in heroic fantasy garb it is possible to canter towards the guns and not shy away from the first or even the second cannonade.

Horace Walpole said that life was a comedy to those that think, a tragedy to those that feel. Since it is fair to guess that the majority of us both think and feel it is fair to expect fiction which appeals to both our thoughts and our emotions. When fantasy attempts to understand the real world, tragic subject matter and comic style can often be the best combination. Byron says in Don Juan: "And if I laugh at any mortal thing/'Tis that I may not weep." But writers must entertain before they have any right to try instruction (even if the only attempt is to instruct the reader's sensibility). Writers have a natural reticence to shout at the same volume the same slogans as those people, quite as miserable and angry as themselves, whose protests at such barbarism as modern war take a more direct and political form. An artist cannot be much of a politician, unless it is during their time off.

If one is primarily concerned with telling a moral tale in the exaggerated form called "fantasy" then comedy can be a big help in relieving what might otherwise be merely a portentous or over-distanced epic narrative. It enables, too, an author to cope with an idea on more than one level. If a writer is working a form where the ironic tone seems largely unsuitable she or he can supply a balance by having a character whose function is to offer an ironic commentary on the protestations and ambitions of the hero. Thus in Leiber Fafhrd is fundamentally gloomy, while the Mouser is fundamentally optimistic. No matter how serious the drama, humour helps humanize the characters. On a simple level the use of humour is the secret of the success of most popular film-thrillers, from *The Maltese Falcon* to *Jaws*, *The Wind and the Lion*, to *The Man Who Would Be King*, even *Raiders of the Lost Ark*. One thing that can be said for *Star Wars* (dreadful though the script was) is that it may well have banished the tone of Awful Seriousness which seemed to overtake even fairly good directors when faced with the prospect of doing quite an ordinary or minor science fiction subject.

To try to distinguish between different forms of humour here would be as silly as trying to define different kinds of fantasy and science fiction. It ranges from the wit of Meredith to the comedy of Dickens.

From Homer onwards the world's epics and fables have given us comic characters, including, of course, the original Conan, the buffoon, companion of Finn and the Red Branch heroes, yet there are surprisingly few such characters in the vast numbers of recent heroic fantasies claiming the mythological romance as their particular heritage. The fantasy comic strips actually offer a wider selection of humour. I would recommend, for instance, the adventures of *Cerebus the Aardvark*.

That comedy and fantasy may combine to delightful effect (as in *A Midsummer Night's Dream*) was shown by *Unknown* where writers like De Camp and Pratt, Anthony Boucher, Fritz Leiber, Henry Kuttner and many others came into their own. It is probably not a coincidence that the best writers have almost all shown themselves capable of producing marvellous comic stories. A strong sense of comedy or irony in genre writers ensures that their chosen genre, at least in their hands, never becomes stale and over-formalized. Chandler and Hammett introduced sophisticated humour into the thriller without for a moment destroying the dramatic power of their work and gave the detective story a lease of life it retains to this day, as well as improving the overall level of aspiration of writers.

> It was from Dando grown very old and ramshackle, that Beliard heard the same story in his childhood, and he was immediately seized by a passionate longing to be nursed by a fairy. His nurse and nursemaids were fairies; his mother, Lady Pervenche, was a fairy of unblemished lineage; he was born into the most distinguished of Elfin courts; he had never seen anything but fairies—and he longed with childish violence to be nursed by a fairy. Now he was grown up, unassuming and short-sighted, but for all that a credit to his upbringing. He had an intermittent ambition to play the flageolet, and used to steal off to the pool of Barenton where he could practice undisturbed.

He was working at the open-pipe octave, where a hoot at the bottom and a squeak at the top are equally hard to avoid, when he heard approaching wings and saw Puck, the old whipper-in of the royal pack of werewolves, and four stout kennel lads carrying buckets, alight by the pool.

Sylvia Townsend Warner, *Beliard*, 1974

One of the few specifically comic series in epic fantasy (if that's what it is) is Terry Pratchett's, beginning with *The Colour of Magic* (1983) which sets out, very successfully, to lampoon the kind of sword-and-sorcery story derived chiefly from Robert E. Howard. Somewhat in the tradition of Pratt and De Camp, Pratchett takes a locale similar to one of Howard's or Leiber's, but where Leiber offers delightful irony, Pratchett gives us broad comedy. It is excellent farce—intelligent entertainment. *The Light Fantastic* (1985) is even better, and there have been many more sequels, all very satisfactory stuff. Here is a sample:

All the heroes of the Circle Sea passed through the gates of Ankh-Morpork sooner or later. Most of them were from the barbaric tribes nearer the frozen Hub, which had a sort of export trade in heroes. Almost all of them had crude magic swords, whose unsuppressed harmonics on the astral plane played hell with any delicate experiments in applied sorcery for miles around, but Rincewind didn't object to them on that score. He knew himself to be a magical dropout so it didn't bother him that the mere appearance of a hero at the city gates was enough to cause retorts to explode and demons to materialize all through the Magical Quarter. No, what he didn't like about heroes was that they were usually suicidally gloomy when sober and homicidally insane when drunk. There were too many of them, too. Some of the most notable questing grounds near the city were a veritable hubbub in the season. There was talk of organizing a rota.

As well as a fair amount of original invention of his own, Pratchett offers us dragons who can only fly a few feet above the ground, incompetent wizards, leaking grimoires, and Hrun the Barbarian:

> Observe Hrun, as he leaps cat-footed across a suspicious tunnel mouth. Even in this violet light his skin gleams coppery. There is much gold about his person, in the form of anklets and wristlets, but otherwise he is naked except for a leopardskin loincloth. He took that in the steaming forests of Howondaland, after killing its owner with his teeth. In his right hand he carried the magical black sword Kring, which was forged from a thunderbolt and has a soul but suffers no scabbard. Hurn had stolen it only three days before from the impregnable palace of the Archmandrite of B'Ituni, and he was already regretting it. It was beginning to get on his nerves.
> "I tell you it went down that last passage on the right," hissed Kring in a voice like the scrape of a blade over stone.
> "Be silent! "
> "All I said was—"
> "Shut up!"

Both irony of Sylvia Townsend Warner's kind and farce like Pratchett's have their place in epic fantasy and must surely be preferable to the interminable diet of princesses, unicorns, talented teenagers, doom-haunted barbarians and evil sorcerers which threatens to turn the form into a less interesting version of *Dungeons & Dragons*.

It seems to me that if fantasy fiction is to avoid the stultification that has befallen, say, commercial sf, it would do well to recall its strong bonds with comedy.

"To love Comedy," says Meredith, in his great essay *On The Idea of Comedy and the Uses of the Comic Spirit*, "you must know the real world, and know men and women well enough not to expect too much of them, though you may still hope for good." To keep a form vital you must draw your inspiration not from other books in that form but from life itself, from experience, from knowledge of men and women, and, where fantasy fiction is concerned, from an enthusiasm for the epic, the myth, the noble metaphor which speaks to us on a hundred levels. And to make such things speak to their fellows in as many voices as possible, writers must employ comedy to remind their readers that no matter how intense the images, how grand the themes, how awe-inspiring the terrors, one is still writing about reality.

5
Epic Pooh

Why is the *Rings* being widely read today? At a time when perhaps the world was never more in need of authentic experience, this story seems to provide a pattern of it. A businessman in Oxford told me that when tired or out of sorts he went to the *Rings* for restoration. Lewis and various other critics believe that no book is more relevant to the human situation. W. H. Auden says that it "holds up the mirror to the only nature we know, our own." As for myself I was rereading the *Rings* at the time of Winston Churchill's funeral and I felt a distinct parallel between the two. For a few short hours the trivia which normally absorbs us was suspended and people experienced in common the meaning of leadership, greatness, valor, time redolent of timelessness, and common traits. Men became temporarily human and felt the life within them and about. Their corporate life lived for a little and made possible the sign of renewal after a realisation such as occurs only once or twice in a lifetime.

For a century at least the world has been increasingly demythologized. But such a condition is apparently alien to the real nature of men. Now comes a writer such as John Ronald Reuel Tolkien and, as remythologizer, strangely warms our souls. Clyde S. Kilby: "Meaning in the Lord of the Rings," *Shadows of Imagination*, 1969

I have sometimes wondered how much the advent of steam influenced Victorian ballad poetry and romantic prose. Reading Dunsany, for instance, it often occurs to me that his early stories were all written during train journeys:

> Up from the platform and onto the train
> Got Welleran, Rollory and young Iraine.
> Forgetful of sex and income tax
> Were Sooranard, Mammolek, Akanax:
> And in their dreams Dunsany's lord
> Mislaid the communication cord.

The sort of prose most often identified with "high" fantasy is the prose of the nursery-room. It is a lullaby, it is meant to soothe and console. It is mouth-music. It is frequently enjoyed not for its tensions but for its lack of tensions. It coddles, it makes friends with you; it tells you comforting lies. It is soft:

> One day when the sun had come back over the forest,
> bringing with it the scent of May, and all the streams
> of the Forest were tinkling happily to find themselves
> their own pretty shape again, and the little pools lay
> dreaming of the life they had seen and the big things
> they had done, and in the warmth and quiet of the
> Forest the cuckoo was trying over his voice carefully
> and listening to see if he liked it, and wood-pigeons
> were complaining gently to themselves in their lazy
> comfortable way that it was the other fellow's fault,
> but it didn't matter very much; on such a day as this
> Christopher Robin whistled in a special way he had,
> and Owl came flying out of the Hundred Acre Wood
> to see what was wanted.
> *Winnie-the-Pooh*, 1926

It is the predominant tone of *The Lord of the Rings* and *Watership Down* and it is the main reason why these books, like many similar ones in the past, are successful. It is the tone of Warwick Deeping's *Sorrell and Son*, of John Steinbeck at his worst, or, in a more sophisticated form, James Barrie (*Dear Brutus,* etc.) and Charles Morgan; it is sentimental, slightly distanced, often wistful, a trifle retrospective; it contains little wit and much whimsy. The humour is often unconscious because, as with Tolkien,* the authors take words seriously but without pleasure:

> One summer's evening an astonishing piece of news reached the Ivy Bush and Green Dragon. Giants and other portents on the borders of the Shire were forgotten for more important matters; Mr Frodo was selling Bag End, indeed he had already sold it—to the Sackville-Bagginses!
>
> "For a nice bit, too," said some. "At a bargain price," said others, "and that's more likely when Mistress Lobelia's the buyer." (Otho had died some years before, at the ripe but disappointed age of 102.)
>
> Just why Mr Frodo was selling his beautiful hole was even more debatable than the price....
> *The Fellowship of the Ring*, 1954

I have been told it is not fair to quote from the earlier parts of *The Lord of the Rings*, that I should look elsewhere to find much better stuff so, opening it entirely at random, I find some improvement in substance and writing, but that tone is still there:

> Pippin became drowsy again and paid little attention to Gandalf telling him of the customs of Gondor, and how the Lord of the City had beacons built on the tops of outlying hills along both borders of the great range, and maintained posts at these points where fresh horses were always in readiness to bear his errand-riders to Rohan in the North, or to Belfalas in the South. "It is long since the beacons of the North were lit," he said; "and in the ancient days of Gondor they were not needed, for they had the Seven Stones." Pippin stirred uneasily.
> *The Return of the King*, 1955

---

*The Silmarillion (1977) is, of course, the finest proof of this argument.

Tolkien does, admittedly, rise above this sort of thing on occasions, in some key scenes, but often such a scene will be ruined by ghastly verse and it is remarkable how frequently he will draw back from the implications of the subject matter. Like Chesterton, and other markedly Christian writers who might be said to have substituted faith for artistic rigour, he sees the petit bourgeoisie, the honest artisans and peasants, as the bulwark against Chaos. These people are always sentimentalized in such fiction because, traditionally, they are always the last to complain about any deficiencies in the social status quo. They are a type familiar to anyone who ever watched an English film of the thirties and forties, particularly a war-film, where they represented solid good sense opposed to a perverted intellectualism. In many ways *The Lord of the Rings* is, if not exactly anti-romantic, an anti-romance. Tolkien, and his fellow "Inklings" (the dons who met in Lewis's Oxford rooms to read their work in progress to one another), had extraordinarily ambiguous attitudes towards Romance (and just about everything else) which is doubtless why his trilogy has so many confused moments when the tension flags completely. But he could, at his best, produce prose much better than that of his Oxford contemporaries who perhaps lacked his respect for middle-English poetry. He claimed that his work was primarily linguistic in its original conception, that there were no symbols or allegories to be found in it, but his Christian beliefs permeate the book as thoroughly as they do the books of Charles Williams and C. S. Lewis, who felt bound to introduce their religious ideas into everything they wrote.

I suppose I respond so antipathetically to Lewis and Tolkien because I find this sort of consolatory Christianity distasteful, a fundamentally misanthropic doctrine. One should perhaps feel some sympathy for the nervousness occasionally revealed beneath their thick layers of stuffy self-satisfaction, typical of the second-rate schoolmaster, but sympathy is hard to sustain in the teeth of their hidden aggression which is so often accompanied by a deep-rooted hypocrisy. Their theories dignify the mood of a disenchanted and thoroughly discredited section of the repressed English middle-class too afraid, even as it falls, to make any sort of direct complaint ("They kicked us out of Rhodesia, you know") least of all to the Higher Authority, their Anglican God who has evidently failed them.

It was best-selling novelists, like Warwick Deeping, who, after the First World War, adapted the sentimental myths (particularly the myth of Sacrifice) which had made war bearable (and helped ensure that we should be able to bear further wars), providing us with the wretched ethic of passive "decency" and self-sacrifice, by means of which we were able to console ourselves in our moral apathy (even Buchan provided a few of these). Moderation was the rule and it is moderation which ruins Tolkien's fantasy and causes it to fail as a genuine romance. The little hills and woods of that Surrey of the mind, the Shire, are "safe," but the wild landscapes everywhere beyond the Shire are "dangerous." Experience of life itself is dangerous. *The Lord of the Rings* is a pernicious confirmation of the values of a morally bankrupt middle-class. *The Lord of the Rings* is much more deep-rooted in its infantilism than a good many of the more obviously juvenile books it influenced. It is *Winnie-the-Pooh* posing as an epic. If the Shire is a suburban garden, Sauron and his henchmen are that old bourgeois bugaboo, the Mob—mindless football supporters throwing their beer bottles over the fence—the worst aspects of modern urban society represented as the whole by a fearful, backward-yearning class for whom "good taste" is synonymous with "restraint" (pastel colours, murmured protest) and "civilized" behaviour means "conventional behaviour in all circumstances." This is not to deny that courageous characters are found in *The Lord of the Rings*, or a willingness to fight Evil—but somehow those courageous characters take on the aspect of retired colonels at last driven to write a letter to the *Times* and we are not sure—because Tolkien cannot really bring himself to get close to his proles and their satanic leaders—if Sauron and Co. are quite as evil as we're told. After all, anyone who hates hobbits can't be all bad.

The appeal of the Shire has certain similarities with the appeal of the "Greenwood" which is, unquestionably, rooted in most of us:

> In summer when the sheves be shene
> And leaves be large and long,
> It is full merry in fair forest
> To hear the fowle's song;

To see the deer draw to the dale,
And leave the hilles hee,
And shadow them in leves green,
Under the greenwood tree.
A Tale of Robin Hood
*(*quoted in *Ancient Metrical Tales*, 1829)

There is no happy ending to the Romance of Robin Hood, however, whereas Tolkien, going against the grain of his subject matter, forces one on us—as a matter of policy:

> And lastly there is the oldest and deepest desire, the Great Escape: the Escape from Death. Fairy stories provide many examples and modes of this—which might be called the genuine escapist, or (I would say) fugitive spirit. But so do other stories (notably those of scientific inspiration), and so do other studies. But the "consolation" of fairy-tales has another aspect than the imaginative satisfaction of ancient desires. For more important is the Consolation of the Happy Ending.
> J. R. R. Tolkien, "On Fairy Stories"

The great epics dignified death, but they did not ignore it, and it is one of the reasons why they are superior to the artificial romances, of which *Lord of the Rings* is merely one of the most recent.

Since the beginnings of the Industrial Revolution, at least, people have been yearning for an ideal rural world they believe to have vanished—yearning for a mythical state of innocence (as Morris did) as heartily as the Israelites yearned for the Garden of Eden. This refusal to face or derive any pleasure from the realities of urban industrial life, this longing to possess, again, the infant's-eye-view of the countryside, is a fundamental theme in popular English literature. Novels set in the countryside probably always outsell novels set in the city.

If I find this nostalgia for a "vanished" landscape a bit strange it is probably because as I write I can look from my window over twenty miles of superb countryside to the sea and a sparsely populated coast. This county, like many others, has seemingly limitless landscapes of great beauty and variety, so far unspoiled by excessive tourism or the uglier forms of industry. Elsewhere big cities have certainly destroyed the surrounding countryside but rapid transport now makes it possible for a Londoner to spend the time they would have needed to get to Box Hill forty years ago in getting to Northumberland. I think it is simple neophobia which makes people hate the modern world and its changing society; it is xenophobia which makes them unable to imagine what rural beauty might lie beyond the boundaries of their particular Shire. They would rather read R. F. Delderfield and share a miserable complaint or two on the commuter train while planning to take their holidays in Bournemouth, as usual, because they can't afford to go to Spain this year. They don't want rural beauty anyway; they want a sunny day, a pretty view.

Writers like Tolkien take you to the edge of the Abyss and point out the excellent tea-garden at the bottom, showing you the steps carved into the cliff and reminding you to be a bit careful because the hand-rails are a trifle shaky as you go down; they haven't got the approval yet to put a new one in.

I never liked A. A. Milne, even when I was very young. There is an element of conspiratorial persuasion in his tone that a suspicious child can detect early in life. Let's all be cosy, it seems to say (children's books are, after all, often written by conservative adults anxious to maintain an unreal attitude to childhood); let's forget about our troubles and go to sleep. At which I would find myself stirring to a sitting position in my little bed and responding with uncivilized bad taste.

According to C. S. Lewis his Narnia fantasies for children, a series of seven books beginning with *The Lion, the Witch and the Wardrobe* and ending with *The Last Battle*, were deliberate works of Christian propaganda. The books are a kind of Religious Tract Society version of the Oz books as written by E. Nesbit; but E. Nesbit would rarely have allowed herself Lewis's awful syntax, full of tacked-on clauses, lame qualifications, vague adjectives and unconscious repetitions; neither would she have written down to children as thoroughly as this childless don who remained a devoutly committed bachelor most of his life. Both Baum and Nesbit wrote more vigorously and more carefully:

Old Mombi had thought herself very wise to choose the form of a Griffin, for its legs were exceedingly fleet and its strength more enduring than that of other animals. But she had not reckoned on the untiring energy of the Saw-Horse, whose wooden limbs could run for days without slacking their speed. Therefore, after an hour's hard running, the Griffin's breath began to fail and it panted and gasped painfully, and moved more slowly than before. Then it reached the edge of the desert and began racing across the deep sands. But its tired feet sank far into the sand, and in a few minutes the Griffin fell forward, completely exhausted, and lay still upon the desert waste.

Glinda came up a moment later, riding the still vigorous Saw-Horse; and having unwound a slender golden thread from her girdle the Sorceress threw it over the head of the panting and helpless Griffin, and so destroyed the magical power of Mombi's transformation.

For the animal with one fierce shudder, disappeared from view, while in its place was discovered the form of the old Witch, glaring savagely at the serene and beautiful face of the Sorceress.

L. Frank Baum, *The Land of Oz*, 1904

Elfrida fired away, and the next moment it was plain that Elfrida's poetry was more potent than Edred's; also that a little bad grammar is a trifle to a mighty Mouldiwarp.

For the walls of Edred's room receded further and further till the children found themselves in a great white hall with avenues of tall pillars stretching in every direction as far as you could see. The hall was crowded with people dressed in costumes of all countries and all ages—Chinamen, Indians, Crusaders in armour, powdered ladies, doubleted gentlemen, Cavaliers in curls, Turks in turbans, Arabs, monks, abbesses, jesters, grandees with ruffs round their necks, and savages with kilts of thatch. Every kind of dress you can think of was there. Only all the dresses were white. It was like a redoute, which is a fancy-dress ball where the guests may wear any dress they choose, only the dresses must be of one colour. The people round the children pushed them gently forward. And then they saw that in the middle of the hall was a throne of silver, spread with a fringed cloth of chequered silver and green, and on it, with the Mouldiwarp standing on one side and the Mouldierwarp on the other, the Mouldiestwarp was seated in state and splendour. He was much larger than either of the other moles, and his fur was as silvery as the feathers of a swan.

E. Nesbit, *Harding's Luck*, 1909

Here is a typical extract from Lewis's first Narnia book, which was superior to some which followed it and is a better than average example of Lewis's prose fiction for children or for adults:

It was nearly midday when they found themselves looking down a steep hillside at a castle—a little toy castle it looked from where they stood—which seemed to be all pointed towers. But the Lion was rushing down at such a speed that it grew larger every moment and before they had time even to ask themselves what it was they were already on a level with it. And now it no longer looked like a toy castle but rose frowning in front of them. No face looked over the battlements and the gates were fast shut. And Aslan, not at all slacking his pace, rushed straight as a bullet towards it.

"The Witch's home!" he cried. "Now, children, hold tight."

Next moment the whole world seemed to turn upside down and the children felt as if they had left their insides behind them; for the Lion had gathered

himself together for a greater leap than any he had
yet made and jumped—or you may call it flying rather
than jumping—right over the castle wall. The two
girls, breathless but unhurt, found themselves
tumbling off his back in the middle of a wide stone
courtyard full of statues.

The Lion, the Witch and the Wardrobe, 1950

As a child, I found that these books did not show me the respect
I was used to from Nesbit or Richmal Crompton, who also gave me
denser, better writing and a wider vocabulary. The Cowardly Lion
was a far more attractive character than Aslan and Crompton's
William books were notably free from moral lessons. I think I would
have enjoyed the work of Alan Garner, Susan Cooper and Ursula
Le Guin much more. They display a greater respect for children and
considerably more talent as writers. Here is Garner:

But as his head cleared, Colin heard another sound,
so beautiful that he never found rest again, the sound
of a horn, like the moon on snow, and another
answered it from the limits of the sky; and through
the Brollachan ran silver lightnings, and he heard
hoofs, and voices calling, "We ride! We ride!" and
the whole cloud was silver, so that he could not look.
The hoof-beats drew near, and the earth throbbed.
Colin opened his eyes. Now the cloud raced over
the ground, breaking into separate glories that wisped
and sharpened the skeins of starlight, and were
horsemen, and at their head was majesty, crowned
with antlers, like the sun.

But as they crossed the valley, one of the riders
dropped behind, and Colin saw that it was Susan.
She lost ground though her speed was no less, and
the light that formed her died, and in its place was a
smaller, solid figure that halted, forlorn, in the white
wake of the riding.

The horsemen climbed from the hillside to the
air, growing vast in the sky, and to meet them came
nine women, their hair like wind. And away they rode

together across the night, over the waves, and beyond the isles, and the Old Magic was free for ever, and the moon was new.
The Moon of Gomrath, 1963

Evidently, Garner is a better writer than Lewis or Tolkien. In the three fantasy novels *The Weirdstone of Brisingamen* (1961), *The Moon of Gomrath* (1963), and *Elidor* (1965), his weakness, in common with similar writers, is his plot structure. In a later, better structured book, *The Owl Service* (1970), he improved considerably.

This deficiency of structure is by no means evident in Ursula K. Le Guin, Gillian Bradshaw or Susan Cooper. For my taste Susan Cooper has produced one of the very best recent sequences of novels of their type (modern children involved in ancient mystical conflicts). They have much of Masefield's *Box of Delights* magic. Her sequence, *The Dark is Rising*, has some fine moments. The strongest books are the title volume and the final volume *Silver in the Tree* (1977), while some of the best writing can be found in *The Grey King* (1975):

> They were no longer where they had been. They stood somewhere in another time, on the roof of the world. All around them was the open night sky, like a huge black inverted bowl, and in it blazed the stars, thousand upon thousand brilliant prickles of fire. Will heard Bran draw in a quick breath. They stood, looking up. The stars blazed round them. There was no sound anywhere, in all the immensity of space. Will felt a wave of giddiness; it was as if they stood on the last edge of the universe, and if they fell, they would fall out of Time... As he gazed about him, gradually he recognised the strange inversion of reality in which they were held. He and Bran were not standing in a timeless dark night observing the stars in the heavens. It was the other way around. They themselves were observed. Every blazing point in that great depthless hemisphere of stars and suns was focussed upon them, contemplating, considering, judging. For by following the quest for the golden

harp, he and Bran were challenging the boundless might of the High Magic of the Universe. They must stand unprotected before it, on their way, and they would be allowed to pass only if they had the right by birth. Under that merciless starlight of infinity any unrightful challenger would be brushed into nothingness as effortlessly as a man might brush an ant from his sleeve.

Ursula K. Le Guin in her trilogy *A Wizard of Earthsea* (1968), *The Tombs of Atuan* (1971), and *The Farthest Shore* (1972), is the only one of these three to set her stories entirely in a wholly invented world. She writes her books for children as conscientiously as she writes for adults (she is a leading and much admired sf author whose work has won many awards). Here is a passage from near the beginning, again with its echoes of Frazer's *Golden Bough*:

On the day the boy was thirteen years old, a day in the early splendor of autumn while still the bright leaves are on the trees, Ogion returned to the village from his rovings over Gont Mountain, and the ceremony of Passage was held. The witch took from the boy his name Duny, the name his mother had given him as a baby. Nameless and naked he walked into the cold springs of the Ar where it rises among the rocks under the high cliffs. As he entered the water clouds crossed the sun's face and great shadows slid and mingled over the water of the pool about him. He crossed to the far bank, shuddering with cold but walking slow and erect as he should through that icy, living water. As he came to the bank Ogion, waiting, reached out his hand and clasping the boy's arm whispered to him his true name: Ged.

Thus was he given his name by one very wise in the use of power.

A Wizard of Earthsea

Lloyd Alexander is another American writer who has had considerable success with his books set in an invented and decidedly Celtic fantasy world, but for my taste he never quite succeeds in matching the three I have mentioned. He uses more clichés and writes a trifle flaccidly:

> The Horned King stood motionless, his arm upraised. Lightning played about his sword. The giant flamed like a burning tree. The stag horns turned to crimson streaks, the skull mask ran like molten iron. A roar of pain and rage rose from the Antlered King's throat.
>
> With a cry, Taran flung an arm across his face. The ground rumbled and seemed to open beneath him. Then there was nothing.
>
> *The Book of Three*, 1964

One does become a little tired, too, of Hern the Hunter turning up everywhere. Another legacy from Frazer. Sometimes he appears in books of this kind almost as an embarrassment, as if convention demands his presence: an ageing and rather vague bishop doing his bit at official services.

There are a good many more such fantasies now being written for children and on the whole they are considerably better than the imitations written ostensibly for adults. Perhaps the authors feel more at ease when writing about and for children—as if they are forced to tell fewer lies (or at least answer fewer fundamental questions) to themselves or their audience.

Among these newer writers, Gillian Bradshaw has produced yet another Arthurian trilogy. This one, however, is written from the point of view of Gwalchmai, the son of the King of Orkney and Queen Morgawse (who might be a sorceress). He encounters the Sidhe, some of whom help him as he journeys to be with King Arthur who is fighting a desperate battle against the Saxon invaders. Bradshaw's writing is clear and vibrant, her story-telling has pace and verve.

She lifted her arms and the Darkness leapt. But she was distant again, and I stood at Camlann. I looked up and saw Lugh standing in the west, opposite Morgawse, holding his arm above the island so that the Queen could not touch it. Behind him was light too brilliant, too glorious to be seen. For a moment I saw these two confronting one another, and then my field of vision narrowed. I saw the island and the figures of armies. I saw the Family and myself in it. The armies began to move, and the sounds of battle arose. I realized that I saw things that were yet to come, and was terrified. I covered my face with my arms and cried, "No more!" And abruptly there was silence.

Hawk of May, 1981

The subsequent books in this sequence are *Kingdom of Summer* (1982) and *In Winter's Shadow* (1983).

Several of the emerging children's novelists actually display more original gifts and greater talent than the majority of those writing ostensibly for adults. In my view Robin McKinley is one of the very best of these. Her *The Blue Sword* (1982) won the John Newbery Medal in 1984 and she is building an excellent reputation. *The Blue Sword* is the first of her Chronicles of Damar. She has a fresh and interesting approach to the genre which immediately makes it into something of her own. Her style is robust, elegant and considered, qualities which are a great relief after so many clunking archaicisms and cuticisms which inhabit the great majority of present-day fantasies. Angharad Crewel, the young woman who is her central character, is far more likeable than the tribe of leggy, slightly awkward, pony-loving teenagers appearing all too frequently in recent fantasies. Again McKinley's writing makes me wish I had been able to read them when I was young. They would have been a wonderful antidote to the Famous Five and the interminable valleys, mountains, lakes and forests of Adventure which was most of what we were offered after Enid Blyton had become an acceptable brand name on all the myriad planes and demi-planes of the English middle-class.

The power that washed over that face, that rolled down the arms and into the sword and shield, was that of demonkind, and Harry knew she was no match for this one, and in spite of the heat of Gonturan in her hand her heart was cold with fear. The two stallions reared again and reached out to tear each other; the white stallion's neck was now ribboned with blood, like the real ribbons he wore in his mane. Harry raised her sword arm and felt the shock of the answer, the hilts of the swords ring together, and sparks flew from the crash, and it seemed that the smoke rose from them and blinded her. The other rider's hot breath was in her face. His lips parted and she saw his tongue: it was scarlet, and looked more like fire than living flesh.
The Blue Sword

After reading a good many of these contemporary fantasy stories I remained impressed by the number of authors of adult books who described their characters as children and the number of children's writers who produce perfectly mature and sensible characters who think and act intelligently. I found myself wishing that the likes of McKinley would choose to do more work for grown-ups. Perhaps the reason they don't is that they find they can, writing for teenagers, preserve a greater respect for their audience. Another variety of book has begun to appear, a sort of Pooh-fights-back fiction of the kind produced by Richard Adams, which substitutes animals for human protagonists, contains a familiar set of middle-class Christian undertones (all these books seem to be written with a slight lisp) and is certainly already more corrupt than Tolkien. Adams is a worse writer but he must appeal enormously to all those many readers who have never quite lost their yearning for the frisson first felt when Peter Rabbit was expelled from Mr. MacGregor's garden:

As Dandelion ended, Acorn, who was on the windward side of the little group, suddenly started and sat back, with ears up and nostrils twitching. The strange, rank smell was stronger than ever and after

a few moments they all heard a heavy movement close
by. Suddenly, on the other side of the path, the fern
parted and there looked out a long, dog-like head,
striped black and white. It was pointed downward,
the jaws grinning, the muzzle close to the ground.
Behind, they could just discern great, powerful paws
and a shaggy black body. The eyes were peering at
them, full of savage cunning. The head moved slowly,
taking in the dusky lengths of the wood ride in both
directions, and then fixed them once more with its
fierce, terrible stare. The jaws opened wider and they
could see the teeth, glimmering white as the stripes
along the head. For long moments it gazed and the
rabbits remained motionless, staring back without a
sound. Then Bigwig, who was nearest to the path,
turned and slipped back among the others.

"A lendri," he muttered as he passed through
them. "It may be dangerous and it may not, but I'm
taking no chances with it. Let's get away."
Watership Down, 1972

Adams's follow-up to this was *Shardik* (1974), better written,
apparently for adults, and quite as silly. It was about a big bear who
died for our sins: *Martyred Pooh*. Later, *The Plague Dogs* (1977)
displayed an almost paranoid conservative misanthropism.

I sometimes think that as Britain declines, dreaming of a sweeter
past, entertaining few hopes for a finer future, her middle-classes
turn increasingly to the fantasy of rural life and talking animals, the
safety of the woods that are the pattern of the paper on the nursery
room wall. Hippies, housewives, civil servants, share in this wistful
trance; eating nothing as dangerous or exotic as the lotus, but chewing
instead on a form of mildly anaesthetic British cabbage. If the bulk
of American sf could be said to be written by robots, about robots,
for robots, then the bulk of English fantasy seems to be written by
rabbits, about rabbits and for rabbits.

How much further can it go?

Of the children's writers only Lewis and Adams are guilty, in my
opinion, of producing thoroughly corrupted romanticism—
sentimentalized pleas for moderation of aspiration which are at the

root of this kind of Christianity. In Lewis's case this consolatory, anxiety-stilling "Why try to play Mozart when it's easier to play Rodgers and Hammerstein?" attitude extended to his non-fiction, particularly the dreadful but influential *Experiment in Criticism*. But these are, anyway, minor figures. It is Tolkien who is most widely read and worshipped. And it was Tolkien who most betrayed the romantic discipline, more so than ever Tennyson could in *Idylls of the King*, which enjoyed a similar vogue in Victorian England.

Corrupted romanticism is as irritating to read as the corrupted realism of the modern thriller. For me, Cabell's somewhat obvious irony is easier to take than Tolkien's more obvious sentimentality. I find William Morris naïve and silly but essentially good-hearted (and a better utopianist than a fantast); Dunsany I find slight but inoffensive. Lewis speaks for the middle-class status quo, as, more subtly, does Charles Williams. Lewis uses the stuff of fantasy to preach sermons quite as nasty as any to be found in Victorian sentimental fiction, and he writes badly. A group of self-congratulatory friends can often ensure that any writing emerging from it remains hasty and unpolished.

High quality escapist fiction usually asks a few questions, offers a few insights. Lin Carter, in his *Imaginary Worlds* (the only book I have been able to find on the general subject of epic fantasy), used an argument familiar to those of us who have met the popular fiction buff who feels compelled to justify his philistinism: "The charge of 'escapist reading'," says Carter, "is most often levelled against fantasy and science fiction by those who have forgotten or overlooked the simple fact that virtually all reading—all music and poetry and art and drama and philosophy for that matter—is a temporary escape from what is around us." Like so many of his colleagues in the professional sf world, Carter expressed distaste for fiction which is not predominantly escapist by charging it with being "depressing" or "negative" if it didn't provide him with the moral and psychological comforts he seemed to need.

Carter dismissed Spenser as "dull" and Joyce as "a titanic bore" and wrote in clichés, euphemisms and wretchedly distorted syntax, telling us that the Pre-Raphaelites were "lisping exquisites" and that Ford Madox Brown (1821-93) was a young man attracted to the movement by Morris's (1834-96) fiery Welsh (born Walthamstow, near London) dynamism and that because Tolkien got a CBE (not a knighthood) we must now call him "Sir John"—but Carter, at least, was not the snob some American adherents are. In an early anthology compiled by Robert H. Boyer and Kenneth J. Zahorski, *The Fantastic Imagination*, we find the following: "In addition to their all being high fantasy, the stories selected here are good literature." Amongst the writers to be found in the volume are C. S. Lewis, John Buchan, Frank R. Stockton and Lloyd Alexander, not one of whom can match the literary talents of say, Fritz Leiber, whose work has primarily been published in commercial magazines and genre paperback series. For years American thriller buffs with pretensions ignored Hammett and Chandler in favour of inferior English writers and here we see the same thing occurring with American fantasy writers. Some of them might be English, but they are not literary writers merely because of that. As often as not they flatter middle-brow sensibilities and reinforce middle-class sentimentality and while they might write a better sentence than the average pulp writer, they are still catering to the popular middle-brow taste.

Yet Tennyson inspired better poets who followed him, who sought the origin of his inspiration and made nobler use of it. Both Swinburne and Morris could, for instance, employ the old ballad metres more effectively than Tennyson himself, refusing, unlike him, to modify their toughness. Doubtless Tolkien will also inspire writers who will take his raw materials and put them to nobler uses. At least recent fantasy, while not exactly in the heroic mode, is moving into the city. For my own part, I would love to believe that the day of the rural romance is done at last. How many more disguises can it wear?

6
EXCURSIONS AND DEVELOPMENTS

SELIM: Do you believe in magic, Hassan?
HASSAN: Men who think themselves wise believe nothing till the proof. Men who are wise believe anything till the disproof.
SELIM: What do we know if magic be a lie or not? But, since it is certain that only magic will avail you, you may as well put it to the test.
James Elroy Flecker, *The Story of Hassan of Bagdad and how he came to make the Golden Journey to Samarkand*, 1922

I've long held the view that category definitions in the arts are destructive both of the thing they try to describe and of the aspiration of the artist. They produce an unnecessary self-consciousness. They are convenient only to over-formalised stock systems and third rate academic discussion.

"Schools" and "movements" exist, usually for very short periods, because conservative and authoritarian elements force individuals to club together against them. A school prolonged past its immediate necessity for existence becomes itself conservative and rigid, producing what you might call false rivalries. Those who learn one particular dialectic find themselves trapped by it. Once a movement comes into vogue it is not unusual for its original adherents to reject it and move to new territory. Artists must constantly reject and then rediscover the past in their search for a vocabulary that is both private and universal; cults, secret languages, enthusiasm for unfashionable, forgotten or "undiscovered" hero-models, displays of dandyism and sensational social and artistic behaviour are all part of the equipment of individuals seeking confidence and assertiveness in a world to which they feel in some ways opposed. The impulse was as common to Pre-Raphaelites as to modern rock music enthusiasts. Fashion, not any particular version of a genre, is our enemy.

"Epic fantasy" is a term as meaningless in the end as "science fiction" but we know roughly what is described by it. It covers a range of fiction from Morris to Harrison. Its proponents often have very different uses for the form. From the 1960s there have been a variety of interventions into it by sophisticated writers who have effectively turned it on its head. It can be rarefied or it can be very crude; humane or misanthropic; "escapist" or "serious." Finally, and with the exception of hacks who seek and purvey the lowest common denominators, it is as varied in expression as the temperaments of those who produce it. We have late flower-power styles on the one hand and comic-book-derived styles on the other. They are good or bad according to who uses them.

Essentially they are all expressions of a second Romantic Revival which began to gather force in the late sixties, with drugs and rock music as its most potent and obvious expression. As with most Romantic movements it has its share of dead heroes: for Keats, Shelley and Byron we can substitute Brian Jones, Jimi Hendrix and Jim Morrison. Perhaps it would be fairer to make comparisons between rock stars and the figures of the Aesthetic movement, like Dowson, Beardsley or even Wilde. The work is wholly different in everything but spirit, of course, but the comparisons are obvious. Epic fantasy struck the public imagination at about the same time as modern rock and roll. The two have coherent points of intersection. There are many obvious examples: bands deriving names and titles of songs from Tolkien, Peake and others, in the sixties there were the "psychedelic" and "heavy metal" science fiction orientated performers. Progressive rock was full of epic fantasy references and on occasions took whole books or series of books as the basis for stage presentations and record albums. Survivors into the present include Pink Floyd, Hawkwind, Blue Oyster Cult, David Bowie and many others. Not only Tolkien has been a source for these performers. We have seen whole record conceptions like *The King of Elfland's*

Daughter. When Rodney Matthews painted the Rolling Stones as worn-out heroes of a sword-and-sorcery story he captured perfectly the important cross-currents of the new romanticism.

It could be that until recently this romantic drive, in politics and the arts, was confined to a relative minority in the West, but with an increase in population, with a majority of that population being young, we are now witnessing an emphatic shift in artistic and literary taste which is bewildering and frightening to those whose opinions were formed in an earlier social climate. They have been sensed and taken up by conventional writers of many genres, especially that of the middle class social novel, which is now as full of mysteriously banging doors, mysterious spectres and empty coffins as any Gothic.

Side by side with an atavistic relish for swords and dragons is an appreciation of the new, rich language of modern life, of the singers, like Bruce Springsteen, who celebrate it in urban romantic images— "Snakeskin suits packed with Detroit muscle..."—of punk heroes who could so easily be the Gray Mouser in black plastic jackets and drainpipe jeans. The West has never at any single time possessed such a wealth of romantic imagery and talent, but it has hardly begun to flower; we could be witnessing only the germinal stages, for there has yet to be developed a literary and visual vocabulary to reflect the impact of so much raw material. We are definitely seeing an upsurge in urban fantasy, borrowing many of the tricks of epic fantasy, in which vast invented cities form the background of the story just as vast invented landscapes were once the staple. Cities where sophisticated magic works hand in hand with steam-run machinery, bizarre flying machines and nostalgic methods of transport. A nostalgia for the past, in fact, remains a feature of these stories, with the battered bricks of abandoned machine shops replacing the old stones of the Gothic ruin, but this in turn allows good writers to turn their work into coherent fables of modern life.

The astonishment of writers of epic fantasy who saw their work gaining a wide audience was something like the feelings experienced by the old black blues-singers of the late fifties who were brought from obscurity in America to England and the Continent to discover that they were heroes to the large audiences waiting to hear them. I went from having a tiny audience primarily of magazine readers to becoming a cult within a few years. Within ten years we saw books originally published in small editions and often remaindered enjoying large sales. This resulted in a revival of fantasy "classics," excellent out of print books of genuine merit, like Eddison's, Leiber's and Anderson's. Side by side with this phenomenon has been the upsurge in sales of calendars, posters and collections of artwork. More and more talented artists have found a market for their work. There has also been an upsurge of talent and ambition throughout the world of the graphic novel. Barry Smith, the quintessential Conan artist, has his own following who buy his beautifully produced posters. Michael Whelan's renderings of Elric have sold steadily over many years, as have the beautiful posters and books issued by Robert Gould. Artists who do strips, posters and book jackets have large fan-followings in their own right. These include Roger Dean, Frank Frazetta, Jeff Jones, Jim Cawthorn, Corben and many, many more.

While in some ways the "Golden Age" of the sixties and seventies, with its proliferation of fantastic posters and full-colour picture books, is over, there is still a constant audience for the best of that work. The imagery itself has worked thoroughly into the fabric of popular culture. Work which seemed new and dynamic in its youth now seems familiar and comfortable. There were some spectacular falls during that transition. Some of the firms, like Big 0, seemed so thoroughly geared to the optimism and sense of wonder that emerged in the sixties that they rose naturally on the crest of a social wave—and crashed dramatically when it struck the economic rocks of the late seventies and early eighties. But private presses continue to do lavish deluxe illustrated editions of "fantasy classics" like *The Dying Earth*, *The Tritonian Ring* and *Black God's Kiss* while recent editions of my own work have received wonderful illustrations. There are a number of minor industries specializing in Howardiana and Tolkieniana (as well as Moorcockiana!). In the case of Conan's creator these high-priced, well-produced books, pamphlets and posters probably make more money for their publishers than Howard ever earned in his entire career.

The success of *Star Wars* meant that more producers and directors became interested in producing unashamedly romantic science fiction and fantasy movies. With the exception of *Lord of the Rings*, few of these have been much good up to now. The old Conan movies were both derivative of bad action movies and of bad books derived and debased from Howard's originals! They very rapidly degenerated into complete meaninglessness—and the public, it seems, objected. After *Red Sonja* (1985) was released in the US and Britain it was scarcely in the theatres long enough for anyone to see it all the way through.

You'll note that I have deliberately resisted discussing the sword-and-sorcery movies which have emerged since the late seventies. Those I have seen have been generally disappointing, whether live action or animation. The people who make the movies seem to have no genuine instinct for the form (as Ford had, for instance, for the Western) and cannot convince an increasingly sophisticated audience. We have progressed naturally, it seems, once again from true Romanticism to the infantile nonsense of Grand Guignol. There are signs, with the success of Tolkien's epic, that this will ultimately change.

I suppose it will not greatly matter if, out of all the subgeneric dross, good things emerge. We have seen the likes of Le Guin, Harrison, Wolfe and Russ make something of their own from the form. Each of these writers is very different in character, style and intention, yet they are all extremely talented. One generation, like McKinley, Goldstein, Greenland, Pratchett, McKillip, and Powers have already established their credentials; another, like VanderMeer, Jeffrey Ford, K. J. Bishop and China Miéville are vigorously moulding the form to their own specific needs. Epic fantasy is proving itself a highly flexible form, perhaps even wider in what it can encompass than most science fiction. Perhaps, in certain forms, it is already the mainstream.

How much fantasy fiction has influenced "mainstream" writers isn't hard to tell. I have seen one of my early Hawkwind albums go from *Warrior on the Edge of Time* to *Woman on the Edge of Time* while Brian Aldiss saw one of his best novels ripped off by a robber baroness and greeted with gasps of admiration by critics, thirty-five or so years after the original had skulked out under a genre cloak. Meanwhile the genre's ambitions themselves have changed. In the forefront of this celebration is M. John Harrrison, supplying the dialectic for this new generation even more successfully than he supplied it for the last. Much of what is published today that is good has close affinities with the work, say, of Harrison or Russ. Certainly

Harrison's is influencing a whole, dynamic new generation, which seeks out the best and embraces it. These are writers who will take the generic elements and turn them into something personal, which bears the mark of an idiosyncratic style, which makes use of language the way, for instance, Robert Nye has done in his pastiche memoirs of Falstaff, Merlin, Faust and Sir Walter Raleigh, or even employ the range of symbolism and structure for more experimental story-telling, as Peter Ackroyd did in *Hawksmoor*, as John Crowley does in such books as *Little, Big* or as Robert Meadley will do in *Return to Ost* when it is finally published. This is a wonderfully original use of the epic fantasy form. It is good to see more women writers bringing their ideas and dynamic to the form. It is, after all, a genre which owes as much to the female novelists of the 18th and 19th centuries as it does to the men. Without Mary Shelley, Clara Reeve, Ann Radcliffe and scores of others, the epic fantasy tale could not exist in its present form.

The influence of the South American "fantastic realists" is showing everywhere, these days. In my view a little more of this influence would do no harm, but I continue to counsel would-be writers of fantasy to give themselves a strict diet of Elizabeth Bowen, Henry Green, Angus Wilson and Elizabeth Taylor for at least a year. They might not want to write the best ever social novel, but they should see how they are written and why they are important. Combative philistinism is a dead end.

It's often argued that a good test of a writer is if he or she is able to make existing conventions seem completely fresh, as if you'd never read them before. So long as it attracts such writers, a genre never really perishes. It can be pronounced dead only to spring to life again, lusher than ever. Genres are always being rediscovered, renamed or re-invented, certainly reinterpreted, and a form with its origins so close to our unconscious, to myth and folklore, will continue to attract talented writers. If I continue to bemoan the fact that most of the stuff published is shallow, imitative, worthless and without genuine resonances, either literary or psychological, it is not to attack what is good, vital, stimulating.

One of the peculiar developments in the past few decades has been the rise of the "Dungeons & Dragons" and "Magic" industries. These role-playing games are derived directly from epic fantasy. They owe everything to the original writers like Howard or Tolkien. Hundreds of thousands of people, mostly teenagers, put in large parts of their lives questing for treasures, outwitting wizards and doing in dragons. I must admit that these games are too complex for me and while they hold no attraction, I am fascinated by the elaborate pains people take in playing them. I also think they teach co-operative problem solving so am not even worried about their social effect. They also happen to sell more books because people are now frequently buying books because they are curious to discover the origins of their favourite game. This industry has led to writers producing books which are essentially templates for role-playing games. Though I've written one elaborate but unproduced role-playing game, it's a subject I'm not qualified to discuss and I am sure there must be a number of books which deal with the phenomenon itself. The kid you see in the street who appears to be the village idiot, might well have a huge IQ. He also happens to "be" Gorijor the Thief, on a dangerous mission to the City of Slithering Salamanders. And that bulge in his pocket doesn't mean his pleased to see you but that he's carrying a sizeable force of toy soldiers, each one of which is a character in a complicated drama being enacted across a district, sometimes an entire county and doubtless, these days, the whole world. What was virtually a formless ambience in my eleven-year-old head is probably a highly codified and fully understood structure in the head of today's eleven-year-old. The impulses are the same, but there are now huge industries (like those which produce all kinds of movie "spin-offs") ready to tap into them, to exploit them commercially, to supply them with rules or information.

Commercial interests, of course, are always in the process of taking away from the people (folk music, the blues), formalizing and sanitizing something and selling it back to them, just as commercial interests successfully institutionalized so much rock music and produced bland, superficial, unthreatening copies of the styles of the great originals. If this continues to happen to epic fantasy, we shall probably experience a typical reaction. Publishers will be found with a great deal of rubbish on their hands which nobody wants. At this stage, publishers usually announce that the genre they have bled white "no longer sells." The difference here is that there already better and more potentially popular writers doing more original things within, or just outside, the genre. I review a few of them as an appendix to this book.

One thing, I think, is certain: this revival of direct and unashamed romanticism will have some sort of profound effect on our culture. Compared to its influence on the popular arts, its influence in literature and painting has been smaller, but it is beginning to show. Ultimately it could have a stronger influence on a new generation than science fiction had on the "pop" painters and novelists who enjoyed their vogue in the fifties and sixties.

For too long now we have experienced the restraints and self-consciousness of a predominantly middle-class, pompously male and cautious literary establishment. We have witnessed—and continue to witness—the folly of discredited academics in music and painting who, finding themselves unable to judge by the standards of previous generations, refuse to judge at all and, as academics always will, look favourably only on work whose styles and motives are easily recognized. Recognition, indeed, is the key word. One feels sorry for many of these thin, parsimonious souls whose opinions will seem so insubstantial. The popular revival of full-blooded, highly disciplined romanticism could turn all their notions upside down.

With new aesthetic standards emerging, new battles must be fought, but in the meantime honest vulgarity is always preferable to hypocrisy and caution. If we must be given stories about talking animals let them at least be sceptical, sardonic and world-weary talking animals. Better still, a book-length romance about a family of ferrets would make a welcome antidote to the sentimental, quasi-romantic drivel presently filling the "Fantasy" sections of our bookshops. ("You'll never guess what's for tea, darlings. It's Pooh-and-Pippin pie!")

But that, I suppose, would be the most unlikely fantasy of them all.

SOURCES

Fairly solid bibliographies of the main writers mentioned in this book can be found in Clute's Encyclopaedias, either of Science Fiction or of Fantasy, as well as in the books of those writers reprinted by Victor Gollacz's Fantasy Masterworks.

Carter's *Imaginary Worlds*, 1973, is a book about epic fantasy. Although academically pretty awful and sometimes downright inaccurate, this book contains an extensive bibliography. It is remarkable, as are most Carter anthologies, for the self-esteem of the author, who never hesitates to mention his own work, no matter how inappropriately! These days, of course, it's possible to get a great deal of academic references to the likes of Tolkien or Le Guin and any good search engine on your computer should get you to your favourites.

For various essays on Tolkien, Lewis and Charles Williams I would recommend the collection edited by Mark Hillegas, *Shadows of the Imagination*, 1969. Another excellent collection (including Dunsany, MacDonald, Tolkien, Lewis, Le Guin, Buchan, Cabell, etc.—as well as a rare and welcome appearance from the Russian, Alexander Grin) is *The Fantastic Imagination*, 1977, edited by Robert H. Boyer and Kenneth Zahorski. The same editors also produced a collection, *Fantasists on Fantasy*, 1984, in which eighteen writers discuss their view of the subject. There are also, from Zahorski and Boyer, *The Fantastic Imagination II*, *The Phoenix Tree* and *Visions of Wonder*, all anthologies, and a great many academic studies of fantasy now, usually, but not always, the work of somewhat unoriginal scholars. I can also recommend *Realms of Fantasy*, 1983, an excellent introduction to most of the major writers of fantasy:

Peake, Howard, Le Guin, Tolkien etc., written by Malcolm Edwards and Robert Holdstock, and the *Elsewhere* anthologies edited by Terri Windling and Mark Alan Arnold. Magazines like *The Third Alternative* also feature websites where you can tune in to your favourite fantasy or sf writers and take part in every kind of discussion. There have been some lively discussions concerning ways of defining the fantasy written by many of the new generation of writers. I suspect the discussions will still be going after the need for a new banner has been passed.

Readers who wish to see or buy the books mentioned here are recommended to the various dealers who specialize in fantasy or science fiction. While it is always worth checking your Yellow Pages to enquire if a bookseller near you specializes in fantasy and sf (many used book shops are increasingly devoting space to these genres), these days, of course, your best choice is in having access to the web so that you can find in print material via sites like Amazon or obscure material via the hundreds of specialist dealers who have set up their brightly coloured stalls in today's marketplace.

Most of the best Gothic romances and other 18th and 19th century fiction mentioned in this book are available in cheap editions from publishers like Everyman, Signet and Penguin. If you are buying it second hand I would recommend the Penguin edition of *Melmoth the Wanderer,* edited and introduced by Alethea Hayter, which is by far the best modern edition available (Penguin, 1977). Regarded by many as the best book on the Romantic Movement in general is Mario Praz's *The Romantic Agony*, 1933, reprinted in a revised edition by Oxford University Press, 1970. I am aware that I have not made much mention of the important influences of either the German or the French Romantic movements. Praz is an excellent source for people wishing to know more about these movements. I would also recommend Alethea Hayter's books, such as *Opium and the Romantic Imagination*; Praz's *The Hero in Eclipse in Victorian Fiction*; and R. D. Spector's collection of shorter work by Walpole, Mary Shelley, Lewis, Reeve, Poe, Hawthorne and Le Fanu, *Seven Masterpieces of Gothic Horror* (which includes a very useful bibliography for someone with access to a decent library).

I would also recommend James Cawthorn's *Fantasy: The 100 Best* (1989 from Xanadu Books).

Books on the French symbolists and the surrealists will also add perspective to the subject. The best general book on the Pre-Raphaelites is probably *The Pre-Raphaelites* by Timothy Hilton (Thames and Hudson), though there are many choices; while the best general book on fantasy illustrators could still be Brigid Peppin's *Fantasy: The Golden Age of Fantastic Illustration* (Watson-Guptill, USA/Carter Nash Cameron, UK).

Readers who look for work by George Meredith, who is mentioned frequently throughout this essay, will have to find most of it in second hand shops. The majority of his work is no longer in print. Ironically there are more books in print about him and his novels than there are novels by him. Usually *The Ordeal of Richard Feverel*, *The Egoist* and *Diana of the Crossways* are available, while Ballantine reprinted the rather mannered and untypical *The Shaving of Shagpat* in their Adult Fantasy series. His late masterpiece which in my view is his crowning achievement, *The Amazing Marriage*, has not been available in a new edition for years. I am surprised that the feminist presses, who have reprinted *Diana*, have not thought it worth republishing this, his most powerful attack on the condition of women in Western society. It is worth seeking out.

Finally, I would recommend *The Exploits of Engelbrecht* by Maurice Richardson. These tales of the Surrealist Sporting Club have little to do with epic fantasy, but are an excellent and extremely funny antidote for anyone suffering a surfeit of dungeons, dragons, unicorns, tremendous quests and irredeemable evil. It was published by Gray Walls Press in 1950, reprinted by John Conquest in 1977, reprinted in a definitive edition by Savoy Books in 2001, and remains fairly elusive (though a search for the Savoy website or on Amazon might be rewarding). Anyone prepared to take the quest in pursuit of it will find themselves well rewarded when they read of "The Night of the Big Witch Shoot" or "The Day We Played Mars."

Michael Moorcock,
London, December 1985
Oxford, July 1987
Point Reyes Station, August 2003

APPENDICES

EPIC FANTASY

REVIEW OF *THE BROKEN SWORD* BY POUL ANDERSON

Two similar books were published in 1954. The first, in the USA, was Poul Anderson's *The Broken Sword*. The second, in the UK, was J. R. R. Tolkien's *The Fellowship of the Ring.* These romances drew on familiar Scandinavian and Anglo-Saxon sources but Anderson's was somewhat closer to its origins, a fast-paced doom-drenched tragedy in which human heroism, love and ambition, manipulated by amoral gods, elves and trolls, led inevitably to tragic consequences.

Reading it as a boy, Anderson's book impressed me so powerfully that I couldn't then enjoy Tolkien's. Both stories involved magical artefacts of great power whose possession inclined the users to drastic evil. Both described Faery as a world of ancient, pre-human races no longer as powerful as they were. Both had characters who quoted or invented bits of bardic poetry at the drop of a rusted helm. Nonetheless, I couldn't take Tolkien seriously. Aside from his nursery room tone, I was unhappy with his infidelities of time, place and character, unconvinced by his female characters and quasi-juvenile protagonists.

Anderson set his tale firmly in the early part of the second millennium, in England's Danelaw, when "the White Christ" was threatening the power of all the old gods. He described how, without witch-sight, one might mistake elvish castles and towns for high, bleak mountains and boulder-strewn fells. He made it easy to believe that Yorkshire limestone could be the sparkling escarpments of Alfheim. His women were as sharply drawn and thoroughly motivated as his men.

What's more, Anderson's Eddic verse was better. Admittedly, he didn't fill his book with maps, chronologies and glossaries. He had no wise all-knowing patriarchs. His only longbeard was sinister old Odin, using all his skills to survive. Anderson's human characters belonged to the eleventh century and were often brutal, fearful and superstitious. Their lives were short. Their understanding of the future was a little bleak, with the prospect of Ragnarok just around the corner. To be on the safe side, even Christian priests accomodated the Aesir.

The Broken Sword opens with a bloody reaving. A land-hungry Dane cruelly destroys a Saxon family. Soon afterwards, riding out under a still, full moon, Earl Imric, ruler of all Britain's elves, encounters a Saxon witch, the sole survivor. The witch craves vengeance against the Danes and tells Imric about the conqueror's new-born, unbaptised baby. Knowing the value of humans, who can handle iron, Imric quickly returns home to create, with a captive troll princess, a changeling he can substitute for the baby he calls Scafloc. Imric thus sets off a chain of terrible events foreshadowed by the gift brought to Scafloc's naming ceremony by the Aesir's messenger, Skirnir. The gift is an ancient iron sword broken into two pieces. Ultimately, the sword must be rejoined. This portends no good for men or elves. Meanwhile, the unwitting Danes name their troll-child Valgard.

The boys grow up. Merry, graceful and brave, Scafloc is a credit to his adopted people. Equally strong, Valgard is a brooding brute. Scafloc becomes Alfeim's darling. Valgard becomes a cruel berserker. Glamoured and seduced by the witch given greater power by Odin, Valgard soon adds fratricide and patricide to his crimes.

With Jacobean relish, Anderson thickens his plot with betrayal, rapine and incest. Our human capacity for love and hate are used to further the ambitions of Aesir and Faery alike. An elvish expedition to Trollheim alerts them to the threat of a troll army massing to destroy Alfheim forever. Valgard discovers the truth of his own origins and joins the trolls. Fatally, Scafloc falls in love with a human woman he rescues from Valgard's clutches. Inevitably, as elves are vanquished, he embarks on a journey to reforge the broken sword. Ultimately all will be defeated by their own passions. At best, any victories will be bitter.

Tolkien's saga reflected the sentiments of sacrifice typical of post first world war fiction. Anderson's seems to echo the existential mood of the West after the second world war. *The Broken Sword* has an atmosphere in common with the best forties noir movies, themselves a reaction to the overblown romantic rhetoric of Nazism. With Peake, Henry Treece and even T. H. White, Anderson influenced a school of epic fantasy fundamentally at odds with inkling reassurances. In 1971, Anderson revised his book and weakened it. Victor Gollancz, who have done such an excellent job with their series of fantasy "masterworks," have had the sense to publish the 1954 original. To read it is to understand much of the origins of an alternate fantasy tradition exemplified today by the likes of Harrison, Pullman and Miéville who reject the comforts of The Lamb and Flag and determinedly stick closer to deeper mythic resonances.

From *The Guardian*

Spaced on the Absurd

Review of *The Velocity Gospel* (Accomplice Book 2) by Steve Aylett

The most influential absurdist to emerge from 1950s science fiction was Robert Sheckley. Books like *Mindswap* and *Dimension of Miracles* furnished Douglas Adams with an entire cabinet of borrowed curiosities. Sheckley remains an inspiration for almost every funny sf and fantasy author writing today but he didn't invent humorous sf. It has a long tradition including Kurt Vonnegut's *Sirens of Titan* (1959), Harry Harrison's *Bill, The Galactic Hero* (1966), Charles Platt's *Garbage World* (1967), the great John Sladek's *The Muller-Fokker Effect (1970)* and David Garnett's *Bikini Planet* (2001). Maurice Richardson's 1950s classic *Exploits of Engelbrecht*, recently republished by Savoy, is a riot of the surreal and the absurd. Lately, as desperately needed antidotes to nerd-friendly space fiction and inklingoid fantasy, writers like David Britton, Rhys Hughes, Jeff VanderMeer and Tim Etchells have set their fiction in invented worlds satirically parallel to our own, inhabited by eccentric characters enthusiastically embracing irrationality and paradox.

One of the best of these new absurdists is Steve Aylett. His early mysteries were like Hammett on bad acid, where fast-talking detectives solved metaphysical crimes and sported weapons firing philosophical concepts rather than bullets. *The Crime Studio*, *Bigot Hall* and *Slaughtermatic* were set in the unlikely world of Beerlight. Last year he published the wonderful *Shamanspace* (Codex Books). In it God was found to exist, causing various parties to seek vengeance against him.

Only An Alligator was the first of a new fantasy trilogy featuring the city of Accomplice, whose map includes the Church of Automata, the Ultimatum Restaurant and the Juice Museum. In it Barny Juno, possessing a useful affinity for large animals, got up the noses of some serious demons, saving himself with the help of his pards Edgy and Gaffer and an amiable shaman, Beltane Carom. The demons and their chief, Sweeney, are as cheerfully demented as the citizens of Accomplice, whose corrupt and greedy mayor is the only organ of government. In *The Velocity Gospel,* its even funnier sequel, though thoroughly thwarted by Barny, Sweeney is still determined to have satisfaction and sends his emissary Skittermite aloft to exact it.

> "Because those bastards are completely covered in skin they think they can deny their insides."
> The sheer architectural extravagance of demonic biology was mostly open to inspection, infernodyne veins and pulsing bile yolk fully visible through wide-flung ribs.

Meanwhile, the unwholesome Gaffer lusts after a mechanical clock and gets sucked into Accomplice's latest radical cult, The Friends of Cyril, originally invented as a public diversion by the Mayor but gathering their own reality. Their creed is contained in the Velocity Gospel. Their slogans appear all over the city: TRY OUR LAYERED MOODS and LET ROAD MURDERS YO YO. Skittermite makes unsuccessful attempts on Barny's vitals, only to be thwarted by his lions and chimps. Barny seeks shamanic advice for his love life (Chloe Lowe or Magenta Blaze?) and receives wisdom which satisfies him but confuses us. You can't afford to skip through Aylett's idiosyncratic eloquence and there's no easy way of further summarising the story without reducing it to something else. So much depends on tone and inference. The plot races as fast as it thickens and reaches its existentialist resolution as Barny shacks with Chloe. "I love it here," are his final words. We're promised more fun ahead.

Reminiscent of Firbank's *The Eccentricies of Cardinal Pirelli* or *Sorrow in Sunlight,* Aylett's language is often the substance, the narrative. You are lost unless you accept the logic of his characters, the sardonic rhythms of his prose. And as with Firbank, you tend to begin an Aylett feeling that you've been dropped into the loony bin's annual party, but after a few pages his weirdly angled vision takes you over. By the end of the book it all seems perfectly logical, while the world around you is definitely askew. This is his genius—if you give him your time, he'll return you solid value, an enjoyable roller coaster ride. But you'll never be entirely sure what you've heard or where you've been....

THE EXPERIENCE OF DREAMS
REVIEW OF *THE ETCHED CITY* BY K. J. BISHOP

Ashamoil, the Etched City, survives in a crumbling world of degenerated civilisations in which rival warlords run businesses based on gun-running and slaving against a background of vast deserts and impenetrable tropical forests. Ancient canals, inhabited by giant snakes, run through jungles where tigers laze on the stones of forgotten temples. Seers, occultists, mediums and shamans exploit the fears and superstitions of Ashamoil's many inhabitants. Dreams and reality are indistinguishable. Landscape and imagery are as important to K. J. Bishop's fantasy as character, but it's a measure of this Australian writer's talent that she is as comfortable with her protagonists as she is with her visions and moral complexities.

The Etched City has all the vitality of a first novel and few of the vices. Any initial meagreness of plot is compensated for by a compelling atmosphere which has something in common with Harrison's Viriconium but more closely resembles Ballard's *The Drowned World* or *The Drought*. Like Ballard's or, indeed, Conrad's, her images possess an authenticity drawn from Australia and the Pacific Rim.

In *New Worlds* (1964), Ballard said that speculative fiction would never achieve maturity until it possessed the moral authority of a literature won from experience. His observation was the nearest thing we had to a policy or a movement. Without doubt Bishop's fiction has earned that authority. Moreover, like Ballard's, her characters often reflect new notions of morality. Up to their chins in murder and crime, they have scant chance of old-fashioned redemption. They aren't looking for it and they don't take it when it's offered.

There's plenty of moral argument in Bishop's book, but not much which is conventional. Her people pursue strange dreams and carry awkward burdens. They are often not sure of their own reality. Characters wonder if the rest of the world is created from their own imagination or if they are the invention of some other individual: *She thinks, therefore I am.*

Bishop avoids rationalising her miracles. We are never certain whether or not some of the more bizarre events of the book are dreams. Dreaming does not negate experience here; it's an addition to her lexicon, sharing something with the films of Bergman or the surrealists, underscoring events. In the last third of this novel I became uncertain whether I was reading about a drug fantasy or an actuality. In *New Worlds* I often argued that we were not, as some contended, getting rid of story but were finding ways of telling as many stories as possible. That is what Bishop is doing here.

Gwynn and Raule might have been lovers. They have served in a failed idealistic revolution and, outlawed, taken work as mercenaries. When they reach Ashamoil, Raule attaches herself as a doctor to a hospital helping the city's victims. Gwynn joins the entourage of Ashamoil's most powerful warlord. Like some Mafiosi, his life involves long periods of whiling away his time with his fellow ⌐cavaliers," drinking, gaming and whoring, intermittently called to sudden, violent action. A sensitive pianist, cynical, pitiless and good at his brutal job, he retains that attractive quality found in the hardboiled heroes of Leigh Brackett, who wrote the lion's share of Hawks's *The Big Sleep* and whose Martian romances featuring Eric John Stark were such an influence on Bradbury (who, in turn, influenced Ballard). A more sophisticated writer, Bishop shows the same cool-eyed versatility as Brackett.

Gwynn has one obsession he comes to pursue: the engraver Bethine Constanzin, with whom he falls, perhaps, in love. Her drawings and etchings are described in some detail. Could this sphinx-like woman be the city's creator? The clues Bishop offers to Beth's identity create a dozen potential stories, but it is up to us to follow them through outside the book. Ashamoil, according to these clues is a city made by art. Is Beth human at all? Is she asking the Sphinx's traditional trick questions, or are we inventing the questions for ourselves?

The last part of *The Etched City* features various reverses for Raule when she is asked to nurse the warlord's son, wounded by Gwynn's friend who in turn Gwynn is ordered to murder. There are reverses, too, for Gwynn and his masters. One of their victims begins to take an astonishing revenge. Flowers blossom in the wounds of dead cavaliers. Beth's work assumes ever stranger forms. The living and the dead become indistinguishable.

The Etched City is worth reading just for these scenes which are amongst the most mystifying and astonishing I have come across in a fantasy. They suggest that, no matter what course Bishop decides to take in future—and she is as likely to write a novel of character as another imaginative novel—she is bound to attract a wide audience for her fiction amongst readers of every taste.

Patterns of Chaos
Review of *White Apples* by Jonathan Carroll

Jonathan Carroll keeps getting better. Considering where he started (*The Land of Laughs*, 1975), that's pretty amazing. An American resident in Vienna for over a quarter of a century, Carroll has a unique and sophisticated vision. In the US his reputation has grown until he is now a literary best-seller.

Carroll's modern morality tales take for granted a metaphysical dimension to our lives and have most in common with the work of authors like Alan Wall or Peter Ackroyd. Whether or not containing supernatural themes Carroll's books always deal with the petty, corrosive crimes we commit against one another.

Like many Carroll novels, *White Apples* is a love story. Here his lovers are Victor Ettrich, recently dead of cancer, and Isabelle Neukor, the woman for whom he left his wife and children. An obsessively skilled seducer, Victor finally renounced all others for Isabelle, only for her to get cold feet about living with him. Now he wants to know how he was resurrected and yet still able to live and function in his familiar world. She seems to have more of the answers than he does.

Isabelle, we learn, played Orpheus, bringing Victor back from Purgatory, thus attracting the fury of Chaos determined to thwart an upcoming rebirth in the nature of the universe. That rebirth will destroy Chaos's newly acquired consciousness. The fate of existence now hangs on the life of their unborn child Anjo who must be taught all his father has learned of Death, much of which Ettrich himself can't seem to recall. While still in the womb Anjo manipulates time long enough to help his mother against the increasingly clever and aggressive attempts of Chaos to destroy the three of them.

Attacking memory and identity, using fear, uncertainty and illusion as its initial weapons, Chaos adopts various human and animal disguises. Attempting to preserve life and mutability, the forces of Law are represented by guardian angel Coco Hallis, a woman Victor meets and apparently seduces in a lingerie shop. She can help him but she's not omnipotent, especially against the increasing power of Chaos.

A beautifully realised notion of God as a mosaic consisting of and created by each of our lives, themselves also comprising a mosaic of experience and memory, is reflected in the method Carroll uses in this book, itself something of a mosaic, moving back and forth in time and space to tell the story and produce its moving epiphany. Always a very subtle writer, Carroll quietly presents resolutions and revelations which should you blink you miss. I was impressed by the sureness of this particular structure; he uses no familiar genre tricks to maintain suspense or mystery, yet still communicates nail-biting concern for the well-being of his central characters and a terrified fear for the fate of the universe.

This originality of structure confirms my opinion that Carroll is in no real sense a genre writer at all. There's a moving scene which in a cruder book would have functioned as a finale but here appears about two-thirds of the way through. Chaos, disguised as innocent visitors, begins to attack the zoo animals who are the protagonists' protectors. The courageous self-sacrifice of these animals as they are horribly destroyed fighting a subtle and disgusting kind of evil serves to demonstrate the ferocious power of Chaos which, endowed with sentience, will use any means to survive, even though the end results of its efforts is the corruption and death of Creation itself.

Moving back and forth between the present and versions of their past, talking to their dead, both Victor and Isabelle make journeys of self-discovery, facing the roots of their own moral cowardice and spiritual weaknesses and, by engaging with them, becoming strong enough to face Chaos's threat and learning how to defend themselves against it. But learning self-defence is only the first step in a struggle which, while never relying on conventional theology, carries echoes of Charles Williams (*The Place of the Lion,* 1931) at his very best.

"You can't change the past," one character observes, "but the past is always coming back to change *you.*" A wise old woman warns, "Never let your past salt your meat for you," helping them gather strength as Chaos grows almost overwhelmingly powerful, adopting increasingly subtle manifestations in its efforts to destroy the child still in the womb.

Impressively, Carroll maintains his questions and tensions to the very last paragraph. Thanks to his clever balance of reality and metaphysics, we can't in the end be entirely certain that virtue will triumph and Chaos be defeated, but we have at least come to believe it a thoroughly possible resolution.

From *The Guardian*

METROPOLITAN DREAMS

REVIEW OF *THE PORTRAIT OF MRS CHARBUQUE* AND *THE PHYSIOGNOMY* BY JEFFREY FORD

On the internet message boards, equivalents of fanzine letter columns once favoured by 1960s sf correspondents, they're discussing how to label recent trends in fantasy fiction. Reaction against this temptation encouraged us at *New Worlds* to promote only individual work and contributors like Peake, Ballard, Aldiss or Disch were never discussed in relation to genre.

A term now surprisingly favoured by some writers normally resistant to the labelling of their own work is "New Weird." It seems to be describing a trend away from traditional rural Tolkienesque fables towards well-written stories with a strong urban focus, an impulse which took mysteries from country house murders into Hammett's mean streeets. It also refers to the kind of supernatural fiction once found in *Weird Tales* magazine and perhaps exemplified by H. P. Lovecraft. It was also favoured by Carnell's *Science Fantasy* magazine and in fact was once called "science fantasy," often a combination of horror story, supernatural adventure and interplanetary fiction. Planet Stories, Startling Stories and Thrilling Wonder Stories also ran this kind of romantic fiction. Leigh Brackett and Ray Bradbury were amongst its best practitioners. The term also refers elliptically to the so-called "New Wave" movement of the 1960s, a form of antirealism exemplified in the UK by the work of Ballard, Disch, Sladek and others and in the US by the rather different work of Delany, Zelazny, Ellison and others. The former was an attempt to take some of the content and method of science fiction and produce a kind of fiction which focussed on contemporary urban life, while the latter was aimed at improving the standards of genre without shedding most of its conventions. *New Worlds* was the chief platform for the UK version and Damon Knight's *Orbit* series and Harlan Ellison's *Dangerous Visions* anthologies were where the US version originally appeared. The UK version generally moved away from interplanetary space to concentrate on contemporary cities and concerns. William Burroughs and Philip K. Dick, both essentially urban writers, were prominent early exemplars of both versions.

Does this metropolitan migration represent a growing maturity in generic fantasy, or is urban romance just a more persuasive escapism? Are our new writers any better prose-honers than, say, Dunsany, Leiber or Vance? Do they turn our eyes towards the resonances of real life more successfully than Mosley's LA or Ballard's Shepperton? As with most new "movements" we are left with a few good examples of whom Jeffrey Ford is one.

Much of Jeffrey Ford's appeal for me is his metropolitan focus. In *The Physiognomy* he offered the Well-Built City, dreamed into existence by a sinister genius. In *The Portrait of Mrs. Charbuque* he imbues New York with all the brooding authority of Alan Moore's London: a Victorian Gothic personality, its topper askew, a mad glint in its eye.

Though celebrated and welcomed as a "New Weird" writer, Ford is precisely an author poorly served by genre labelling. His imagination flourishes best on its own alienated turf. If *The Physiognomy* is fantasy of the mind, the fantasy in *Mrs. Charbuque* is mostly in the mind. It's 1893. Piero Piambo, a highly fashionable portraitist, seriously wondering if he's lost his way as a painter, is offered a bizarre commission. A blind man offers him the chance to paint the mysterious Mrs. Charbuque on condition she remains seated behind a screen and Piambo is never allowed to see her. The proposed fee is enormous and will free him to return to his true Muse again. So he accepts. Her beautiful voice tells him he can ask almost any question and she will answer. If he pursues her identity he will suffer dreadfully. He gradually learns her extraordinary life, first as a child when her father perfected a devise for capturing and comparing snowflakes, finding at last two which were, impossibly, identical, then as a drawing room psychic, never revealing her face but apparently possessed of ape-like appearance, possibly married to a jealous husband.

The Physiognamy symbolises its narrator's confusion between identity and place, investigating physical emblems of the inner life and much of *Mrs. Charbuque's* detail is emblematic of Piambo's own problems of authenticity and mystery, his self-deceptions. The city becomes a reflection of his spiritual angst. Puzzling on the execution of his commission, he wanders New York's streets, encountering one grotesque after another, several from his own past, his obsession with his subject growing the more he discovers about her. We learn of Mrs Charbuque's international adventures as a professional oracle. Piambo's beautiful actress mistress becomes involved. His failings of courage and integrity are highlighted. Few characters are as they first appear. A mysterious plague terrifies the city. Is it the creation of a madman, bent on killing all the women he's ever known? Remorselessly the story leads towards Piambo's destruction. Piambo's own life is ultimately spread on the altar of his subject's ego. The astonishing resolution of the increasingly complex Victorian plot is redemptive but opens further moral questions. Will he survive?

The Physiognamy, which won the 1998 World Fantasy Award, equally displays Ford's assured versality, his taste for the absurd, his surreal wit. Like Alan Wall's *The Lightning Cage* it references the more discredited scientific reasoning of an earlier age. In contrast to the actuality of Piambo's New York, Ford's earlier parable invents a world where Physiognamy is elevated, much as the Nazis elevated it, to a precise science, where character, criminal tendencies, even a person's potential future, can be divined through measuring and studying their physical features. Revelations come rich, strange and bleakly funny as the secrets of the Well-Built City and its creator are disclosed. Like Piambo, Physiognamist Cley only reluctantly faces the truth ultimately revealed to him.

If *Mrs Charbuque* invokes *Jekyll and Hyde*, *The Physiognamist* is reminiscent of Lindsay's classic *Voyage to Artcturus,* in which a storm of moral questions are raised and debated. They defy labelling. In both these very different, deeply engaging, novels Jeffrey Ford is courageously, categorically and consistently himself.

From *The Guardian*

Romantic Disciplines

Review of *Perdido Street Station* by China Miéville

Imaginative fiction which refused to rationalise its flights of fancy as dreams, visions or scientific speculation used to be called simply "fantasy." The description suited books as varied as Grant Allen's *The British Barbarians*, Wells' *The Wonderful Visit*, Garnett's *Lady Into Fox*, Woolf's *Orlando*, White's *Mistress Masham's Repose*, Peake's *Titus Groan*, Richardson's *Exploits of Engelbrecht*, Carter's *The Magic Toyshop*, Amis's *The Alteration*, Harrison's *In Viriconium*, Ackroyd's *Hawksmoor*, or Rushdie's *Satanic Verses*.

Today Tolkien-cloned Fantasy has becomes a bookshop category like Mysteries or Romance. We know it has something to do with talking animals, elves, heroic quests or, if we're lucky, comical wizards but we have a problem distinguishing the individual, the literary, from the popular generic.

We once emphatically described J. G. Ballard as *speculative* fiction rather than science fiction because we needed to distinguish his work from a public perception, in spite of Kingsley Amis's puritan prescriptions, that sf was all spaceships, purple people eaters and pulp plot lines. An impression, of course, which TV and movies have confirmed a millionfold since *New Maps of Hell* was published in 1960.

It's currently fashionable to call an unrationalised fantasy a parallel- or alternate-world story, terms borrowed from sf. Such stories began as ideas rather than backgrounds. The best known modern example is probably Philip K. Dick's *The Man in the High Castle* (1962), which proposed a present in which the Allies lost the second world war. Saki did it best, for my taste, in *When William Came* (1914), written before his death in the trenches, about Germany winning the first world war and a British ruling class coming to terms with its conquerors. In the hands of desperate professional writers this device quickly becomes an easy way of tarting up some shabby old plots. The exotic lost land adventure, which began with Defoe, if not with *Palmerin of England*, suffers badly from actual exploration. Mapped, logged and claimed, the mysterious becomes merely untrue. *She* or *Tarzan of the Apes* can no longer exist in the Africa we now know. They can, however, plug on happily in a "parallel" Africa, where the sun never set on the Empire, some Ruritania, or even Dickensian London.

A more ambitious kind of fiction creating a mysterious city or world, such as Gormenghast, has considerable irony and is only a shade away from Faulkner's Yawknapatawpha in intention and sensibility. This fiction tends to use its backgrounds as part of its narrative structure. The best is M. John Harrison's *Viriconium* sequence, which indulges a Walpolean taste for the exotic and the antique. It's a romantic, knowing, post-modern version of the Gothic in which strange, ruined cities are not merely given soul, but achieve sentience, even senility. An often overlooked example is Brecht's *Threepenny Novel,* which offers a marvellously distorted Edwardian London. More recently there's Steve Beard's *Digital Leatherette*. Beard was published beside Miéville, Steve Aylett and Tim Etchells in last year's *Britpulp* anthology edited by Tony White. All borrow elements from popular fiction, have their own invented worlds, with their own architecture, own history and own bizarre inhabitants. Aylett's absurdist thrillers (*Slaughtermatic, The Inflatable Volunteer*) mostly happen in the city of Beerlight, while Etchells's sardonic fables are set in Endland, a world of infinite rundown housing estates, boozers and fast food restaurants.

Like Alan Moore's or Grant Morrison's popular graphic stories, this fiction shares a Shelleyan suspicion of church and state. While finishing China Miéville's impressive second novel, set in the baroque, brooding, gaslit industrial city of New Crobuzon, it became clear that he had a lot in common with the 14th century muralist who decorated our local Oxfordshire church with pictures of the poor and meek ascending to heaven while the authorities, including kings and bishops, went headfirst into the maws of demonic beasts.

Miéville's first novel, *King Rat*, published last year, was an extraordinarily vivid, tactile tale of underground London. Set in the here and now, with subtle hints of the supernatural, it showed the author's genuine empathy for creatures you would normally hope to poison. *Perdido Street Station*, a massive and gorgeously detailed parallel-world fantasy, offers us a range of rather more exotic creatures, all of whom are wonderfully drawn and reveal a writer with a rare descriptive gift, an unusually observant eye for physical detail, for the sensuality and beauty of the ordinarily human as well as the thoroughly alien.

By Chapter One Miéville's graphically convinced us of the mutual sexual passion of a plump human chemist and his sculptor beetle mistress. By Chapter Two we're feeling the pain of a proud hawkperson from the distant desert who has committed some abominable flock-crime and has had his wings sawn off in punishment. His yearning elegaic voice becomes one of the most successful narrative threads in the book. When Miéville avoids generic plotlines and stock characters and writes about individual alienation and love, about difficult relationships and complex architecture, the book comes most thoroughly to life and takes on tremendous tensions.

Perdido Street Station (the name of the rail hub where vast numbers of lines meet) has a wonderfully emblematic setting in its vast, murky, steam-driven Victorian city, teeming with races and species of bewildering variety, in which electricity doesn't exist, where magic works, elementals are part of everyday life, where Hell is an actual place and corrupt politicians make deals with Satan. There are spectacularly gripping scenes with genuinely terrifying fabulous beasts which stop you from eating or sleeping while you read and give you nightmares when you stop. There's a monstrous threat. A noble victory. Yet Miéville's determination to deliver value for money, a great page-turner, leads him to add genre borrowings which set up a misleading expectation of the kind of plot you're going to get and make individuals start behaving out of character, forcing the author into rationalisations at odds with the creative, intellectual and imaginative substance of the book.

That aside, Miéville's catholic contemporary sensibility, delivering generous Victorian value and a well-placed moral point or two, makes *Perdido Street Station* utterly absorbing and you won't get a better deal, pound for pound, for your holiday reading!

From *The Guardian*

Mern Peake

FOREWORD TO *VAST ALCHEMIES* BY G. PETER WINNINGTON

People who didn't know him very well were fond of saying Mervyn Peake's books were so dark, so complex, that writing them had sent him mad. Others, who perhaps knew him a little better, understood that what Peake was writing about was his own life and observation and that he was one of the most deeply sane individuals you could hope to meet, with a wicked sense of humour and a tremendous love of life. He was conscripted in the Second World War, was in London a great deal during the Blitz and was the first War Artist into Belsen. He, like most of us, somehow stayed thoroughly sane, if a little overwrought, throughout the experience. His practical jokes, sometimes concocted with Graham Greene, were often elaborate and subtle. He was inspiring, joyful company whose tragedy was not in his life or work but in whatever ill-luck cursed him with Parkinson's Disease. Increasingly unable to draw or write, he was by the mid-1960s in the last stages of his illness and his public reputation had vanished.

If there's an unsung hero of Mervyn Peake's life and career it has to be Oliver Caldecott, painter and publisher, who became head of the Penguin fiction list in the mid-1960s, founded Wildwood House and died prematurely. Olly and Moira Caldecott, South African exiles, had been friends of mine for several years and we shared a mutual enthusiasm for Mervyn Peake's *Titus Groan* sequence. We'd made one or two earlier efforts to persuade its publisher to reprint it, but were told there was no readership for the books. Caldecott wouldn't give up hope.

I'd been instrumental in getting a couple of Mervyn's short stories published and ran some fragments of fiction and drawings in my magazine *New Worlds*, some of his poetry was still in print, together with one or two illustrated books, but he was thoroughly out of fashion, his reputation not helped by Kingsley Amis describing him "as a bad fantasy writer of maverick status" or my friend Bonfliglioli's dismissal that he was "all wight, Mike, if you like your darkness uttah" and a tendency for those who trawled the margins to link him with the authors of horror stories and hobbit books. He was not served by comparisons with Tolkien because he was Tolkien's antithesis. Peake wasn't producing comfy fairy tales for grown-ups. Peake was a fascinated explorer of human personality, a confronter of realities, a narrative genius able to control a vast range of characters (no more grotesque than life) in the telling of a complex narrative, much of which is based around the ambitions of a single, determined individual, whose rise from the depths of society (or "Gormenghast" as it is called) and extraordinary climb and fall has a monumental, Dickensian quality which keeps you reading at fever pitch. The stuff of solid, grown-up fiction, if you like. It was written by a real poet, with a real relish for words and a real feel for the alienated. Closer to the best Zola than any Tolkien or the generic tosh which followed him.

A fine painter, illustrator, poet and novelist, Peake had been a sunny, bouyant source of life for so many who knew him. He was the opposite of gloomy. His optimism could be unrealistic, but he was never short of it. He was horribly attractive, with his Celtic good looks and sense of style. Though he'd always supported his family, he'd never had much of a knack for making money—he received five pounds for the entire set of illustrations to *The Hunting of the Snark*. Knowing little of the brain in those days—this was before Alzheimer's or Parkinson's were identified—we watched helplessly as Mervyn steadily declined into some mysterious form of dementia while the surgeons hacked at his frontal lobes and further destroyed his ability to work and reason. The frustration felt terrible. His instinctive intelligence, his kindness, even his wit flickered in his eyes, but were all trapped, inexpressible. Here was an extraordinary man being destroyed from within while his genius was rejected by the literary and art world of the day. When critics like Edward Mullens tried to write about Peake, editors would turn the idea down. I had only a modest success. The story, even then, was that Peake had lost his mind. The strain of writing such dark books. That story was a damaging nonsense which continued to be recklessly perpetuated by an acquaintaince, Quentin Crisp, for whom Peake had once illustrated a small book.

The last novel of the sequence, *Titus Alone*, had indeed contained structural weaknesses which we had all assumed were Mervyn's as his control of his work became shaky. One afternoon, however, the composer of the musical setting for *The Rhyme of the Flying Bomb*, Langdon Jones, was leafing through the manuscript books of the novel, which Maeve Peake had asked him if he'd like to see, when he realised that much of what was missing from the published book was actually in the manuscript. Checking further, he found that the book had been very badly edited by a third party, and whole characters and scenes cut.

Jones began to check handwritten manuscript against typed pages and the final typed manuscript, slowly restoring the book to its present much improved state. It took him over a year. He was never paid for the work. We suggested to the original publisher that they republish the book, perhaps with the new text. Not only did they not want to publish the books themselves, they were anxious to hide the fact that the last book had been so badly butchered. They became distinctly negative about the whole thing. I proposed to Maeve that we begin the process of getting back the rights. Meanwhile Mervyn became increasingly unwell.

Oliver said mysteriously that he was hoping to get a new job, which might make it easier to publish the books. And then one morning he phoned me to tell me, with considerable glee, that he was now the guy who was "going to pick the Penguins." And, of course, our first action must be to sort out the *Gormenghast* books and decide how to get them back into print.

Needless to say, the moment Oliver showed interest from Penguin, the original publisher began to see a new value in the books. They were still very reluctant to do a new edition of *Titus Alone*, however. Eventually the whole project was taken over by Oliver, who proposed illustrating the novels from Mervyn's own notebook drawings of his characters. He had the authority and experience to get what he wanted. The new hardbacks were simply versions of the characteristically set Penguin texts prepared by Jones. Anthony Burgess, another Peake fan, contributed an introduction to *Titus*

Groan, which he treated as a classic, and Caldecott brought the three volumes out as Penguin Modern Classics. It was the perfect way to publish the books, boldly and unapologetically, in the best possible editions Mervyn could have.

Next, with the considerable help of my ex-wife, Hilary Bailey, Maeve Peake was persuaded to write her wonderful memoir of Mervyn, *A World Away*, which Giles Gordon, another Peake fan, then at Gollancz, published with enthusiasm. *Monitor* did a rather Gothic TV programme on him. Peake was back before the public at last. Too late, unfortunately, to realise it.

The rest is more or less history. A history spotted with bad media features about Mervyn which insist on perpetuating his story as a doomed one, when in fact it was a very happy story for many years, which perhaps made his tragedy all the more poignant. Bill Brandt shows him as a glowering Celt, a sort of unsodden Dylan Thomas, and his romantic good looks help to project this image. But it's worth remembering that Mervyn could be a cruel and very, very funny practical joker and his home life was about as ordinary and chaotic as the usual bohemian family's. A wonderful father, considerate husband, he was deeply loved by his family and his friends, but he was neither a saint nor a satanic presence and what was perhaps so marvellous for me, when I first went to see him in Wallington, was realising that so much rich talent could come from this pleasant, rather modest, witty man. I was in no doubt, though, that I'd met my first authentic genius. He and Maeve continue to be missed, but that genius is still with us, his children and grandchildren continue to reveal his inheritance, both in character and talent, and his great *Gormenghast* sequence remains the peak, without doubt, of a glorious and generous career.

Peake had a huge, romantic imagination, a Welsh eloquence, a sly, affectionate wit and his technical mastery, both of narrative and line, remains unmatched. Avoiding speculation and sentimentality, G. Peter Winnington, whose own *Peake Studies* journal has charted Peake's career for many years, gives us not just a solid introduction to the author but a considerably better understanding of the man. This book is very welcome.

FACING THE CITY

REVIEW OF *VENISS UNDERGROUND* BY JEFF VANDERMEER

The modern school of urban fantasy whose best writers include Steve Aylett (Beerlight, Accomplice), K. J. Bishop (Ashamoil), Tim Etchells (Endland), Jeffrey Ford, M. John Harrison (Viriconium), China Mieville (New Crobuzon) and others, has also given us Jeff VanderMeer. His Ambergris novel *City of Saints and Madmen* will be published in the UK soon. VanderMeer has worked as an editor, publisher (Leviathan, Ministry of Whimsy) and publicist helping promote the fiction of his contemporaries. His own talent was acknowledged in 2000 with a World Fantasy Award. In the US this year he had an unexpected runaway success with his amusing *Thackeray T. Lambshead Pocket Guide to Eccentric and Discredited Diseases*, which he edited with Mark Roberts.

Urban fantasy appeals to readers not merely seeking escape but looking for versions of their own experience. Its heroes include the likes of Mervyn Peake and Clark Ashton Smith, and in many ways it is the gritty opposite of the Tolkien school, rather as Hammett and Chandler differed from the likes of Christie and Sayers whose isolated country houses supplied the conservative comforts now offered by the stereotypical ranks of "fat fantasy" still stuffing the generic shelves of chain bookshops.

Veniss Underground reflects VanderMeer's generosity towards other writers including the late Edward Whittemore, author of the *Jerusalem Quartet*. Quin, a mysterious and satanic figure who dominates this, VanderMeer's first UK book, is a direct reference to Whittemore's earlier *Quin's Shanghai Circus*.

In VanderMeer's fiction not only people but entire cities re-invent themselves:

Back a decade, when the social planners ruled, we called it Dayton Central. Then, when the central government choked flat and the police all went freelance, we started calling it Veniss—like an adder's hiss, deadly and unpredictable. Art was Dead here until Veniss. Art before Veniss was just Whore Hole stuff, street mimes with flexi-faces and flat media.

The book has three protaganists, twins Nicholas and Nichola and their friend Shadrach, who is Nichola's rejected lover. In the shadows lurks the sinister figure of arch-genetic scientist and Dr. Moreau figure, the mighty Quin, who supplies the government of Veniss with its servants—modified meercats and "Ganeshas" (multi-limbed miniature elephants) employed as couriers, checkpoint guards and so on. Quin might also be the twins' creator. He is certainly Shadrach's employer.

Nicholas, a depressive loser whose own artwork has been stolen by thugs, goes to visit Quin hoping to bargain for a meercat. He disappears. Nichola seeks out Shadrach to help her find her lost brother and becomes the surprised recipient of her own meercat, apparently a gift from Quin. When she in turn vanishes, Shadrach, at once empowered and hampered by his obsessive love for her, becomes determined to seek her out, journeying deeper and deeper into Veniss's below-city levels, using his own connections to Quin to help him in his quest which increasingly takes on the aspect of a Dantesque journey; his Eurydice to Nichola's Orpheus.

The narrative is offered in three main parts from the three characters' viewpoints and is written in first, second and third person, which would seem tricksy in a less talented author. VanderMeer pulls it off effortlessly, solving technical difficulties so well that you are hardly aware of the transitions.

Gradually we learn Quin's diabolical plan, and it is a measure of VanderMeer's talent that his villain, like Milton's Lucifer, is a creature to whom you can't be altogether unsympathetic. Indeed, for a while you find yourself pretty much on Quin's side. There is a scene, in the secret retreat the scientist has created, where the meercats watch recreations of human bestiality and cruelty, learning the worst about the people they ostensibly serve. You emerge from the experience thinking pretty much the same as the meercats, and a suggestion that Quin is deliberately breeding the human race's successors doesn't seem a bad one at all. As the book progresses, these visionary episodes come thicker and faster, and at times the author only barely controls his own invention, hitting his characters with revelation upon revelation, all the while echoing the corruptions and achievements of our familiar world.

The phantasmagoria grows increasingly to resemble a tableau by Bosch, a nightmare vision which shows off VanderMeer's many virtues—his linking of character and plot to the mythic core of his story, his idiosyncratic inventions which derive straight from the psyche, rather than from any generic inspiration, his ambitious style and his vivid descriptive powers. The denouement is as powerful as any I have read.

This is a short, rich book which another writer might easily extend to a bulky trilogy and is a welcome change from the huge tomes which still form a wall between the curious reader and the best of contemporary visionaries like VanderMeer, who could well be creating one of the dominant literary forms of the twenty-first century.

From *The Guardian*

AN AFTERWORD

BY JEFF VANDERMEER

"Believe me, pards, we're living in an age of myths and miracles."
- from *King of the City* by Michael Moorcock

If you've read *Wizardry & Wild Romance* before turning to this afterword, you will have already recognized the book's many virtues. Primary among these, Moorcock, more than most writers I know, achieves a balance between heart and head. In *Wizardry*, Moorcock's passion is matched by a good humor (including barbs that are somehow generous enough to make the point without being sarcastic), and the examples and analysis to back up his assertions. His passion becomes our passion, so that even when (or if) we disagree with his conclusions or his slant on a particular author or book, it is difficult not to agree *while reading his words on the page*.

The passion draws you in, but it is the evidence Moorcock presents that forces you to consider his position. When he calls Lovecraft an "inadequate describer of the indescribable," it's both funny and true, his position shored up through use of well-chosen excerpts. When he points out that Fritz Leiber's Gray Mouser stories are superior to comparable material by L. Sprague De Camp, among others, you immediately understand why because Moorcock has grounded his discussion in analysis of their predecessors.

Moorcock is also not afraid to take on sacred cows. Not having revisited Winnie the Pooh or The Narnia Chronicles for quite some time, I was struck by how much I agreed with Moorcock on their inadequacies—in part because careful excerpts from both series make deficiencies glaringly obvious, in part because Moorcock provides alternatives (like Susan Cooper's *The Dark Is Rising* series) that seem infinitely more interesting to me as an adult.

Moorcock's unique juxtapositions and re-appraisals of writers seem crisp, reasonable, and well-argued, while his theories on epic fantasy are unusually insightful. Moorcock's ruminations on the importance of setting to fantasy—the way in which setting becomes a kind of character—has a usefulness to more than just the reader of fantasy. Writers who include fantastical elements in their work, or hope to rise above genre tropes, would be well-advised to read and re-read that section.

One of the statements in *Wizardry & Wild Romance* that most resonates with me is:

> Their work may be judged not by normal criteria but by the "power" of their imagery and by what extent their writing evokes that "power", whether they are trying to convey "wildness", "strangeness" or "charm"; whether, like Melville, Ballard, Juenger, Patrick White or Alejo Carpentier, they transform their images into intense personal metaphors.

Too often, reviewers, writers, and readers fail to understand the vital link between resonant imagery and characterization, the way in which the landscape is not just a reflection of the writer's concerns, but also those of the main character. Further, the (understandable) emphasis on characterization that typifies modern fiction sometimes robs us of the ability to fully appreciate the other virtues of a story or novel.

I also find Moorcock's comments on the use of humor instructive and important, particularly:

> Comedy, like fantasy, is often at its best when making the greatest possible exaggerations whereas tragedy usually becomes bathetic when it exaggerates. Obviously there is a vast difference between, say, Lewis Carroll and Richard Garnett but the thing that all writers of comedy have in common is a fascination with grotesque and unlikely juxtapositions of images, characters and events: the core of most humour, from

> Hal Roach to Nabokov… Jokes are not Comedy and
> stories which contain jokes are not comic stories.
> The art of ironic comedy is the highest art of all in
> fiction and drama but it is by no means the most
> popular art.

Although Moorcock has always known this to be true, it is a truth that many popular writers today, even those already into their early thirties, may not recognize until too late. Beyond "irony," "unlikely juxtapositions," and "exaggerations," humor, or comedy, especially of the black variety, allows the true seriousness of a story or novel to strike home. To be without this element is, in a sense, to be a body without a vital organ.

Each of you will have your favorite sections of this book, sections that speak to you personally. However, although the sections on landscape/imagery and humor spoke on an intimate level to me, it is difficult for me to select one essay over another, because of the two separate but equally compelling ways in which they acted upon me. In the first case, some essays brought me knowledge and insight I lacked before. In the second case, Moorcock clarified and brought into focus thoughts and ideas I had had before reading *Wizardry & Wild Romance*. To be both validated and taught by a book is a wonderful experience.

Still, I did have two regrets after reading this book. First, that Moorcock's skillful depictions of and excerpts from some of my favorite books brought back a kind of nostalgia for a mythic age of First Reading now long past…and thus the regret that some books are forever lost to me because of the vagaries of time and experience.

Second, and more importantly, I regret that Moorcock's authoring of *Wizardry & Wild Romance* precluded him from using some of his own work as exemplary of the best of epic fantasy, or fantasy in general. (It might not have stopped another author, but modesty is among Moorcock's many virtues.)

As a result, and through no fault of Moorcock's own, *Wizardry & Wild Romance* is, by definition, incomplete. Moorcock's presence permeates it at a sub-atomic level, yet he is not allowed to take up his proper place in its hierarchy.

The world certainly does not suffer from a lack of writings about Moorcock's work, and an afterword cannot hope to compete with such works. However, it is worth reminding ourselves just how pervasive, how ubiquitous, Moorcock's presence has been for more than forty years. (That very quality—of dependability and excellence over a long career—creates a sense of familiarity too close to taking him for granted.)

Whether as editor for *New Worlds*, and champion of the New Wave, or as a writer who benefited from the influence of both the grittiest pulps and the loftiest canonical literature, Moorcock has consistently demonstrated a talent equal to his ferocious ambition. This talent has taken so many forms that it seems there must surely be several Moorcocks, not just one. It is difficult, perhaps, to reconcile the writer of the Elric stories with the writer of *Mother London* (until you recognize the primacy of the individual over systems that has been the one constant in all of Moorcock's fiction), and yet both are exemplary of their type. From the sublime, complex *Gloriana* to the brilliant, funny Dancers at the End of Time series, to the audacious, controversial Pyat books, Moorcock has never shied away from a constant exploration of genres—usually by exploding or subverting them (or by writing outside of genre altogether).

As Angela Carter famously wrote in the *Guardian*, in her review of *Mother London*:

> Posterity will certainly give him that due place in the
> English Literature of the late twentieth century which
> his more anaemic contemporary begrudges; indeed,
> he is so prolific that it will probably look as if he has
> written most of it anyway.

As to the question of influence, this book itself is evidence of that influence. Since its original publication in the 1980s, *Wizardry & Wild Romance* has long been cited by critics, readers, and writers as an important text. It has been taught in universities, referenced in several critical studies, and been appreciated by those general readers for whom it provides a compass, or map, into epic fantasy.

It is also no coincidence that appreciations of Moorcock on the occasion of his sixtieth birthday came from such diverse sources as

Peter Ackroyd, Brian Aldiss, Jonathan Carroll, David Britton, Andrea Dworkin, William Gibson, and Iain Sinclair. Carroll's appraisal of Moorcock represents a common sentiment among many from his generation: "If there were a Mount Rushmore for writers, he'd be on it. I would kill to have written some of the books he's written."

Promising younger writers also continue to be influenced by Moorcock, including K. J. Bishop, China Miéville, and Rhys Hughes. Hughes, in particular, points to Moorcock's protean talent as to why the man has been so influential, and says it in a way I can't better:

> I guess the most important things I admire about his work are its broad scale, vast range, technical invention, its generosity, its refusal to market or expound a political or religious system, its rare willingness to accept humans as they are (saturated with contradictions and paradoxes), its love of life *as it is*, coupled with a blistering social and philosophical conscience, its energy and drive, its wit and color and richness.

But perhaps the observation most relevant to *Wizardry & Wild Romance* occurs in *Supernatural Fiction Writers: Contemporary Fantasy & Horror*, edited by Richard Bleiler: "While many of his contemporaries seem intent on narrowing down the outside world to fit their opinions and desires, [Moorcock] prefers to expand himself in an attempt to fill the world."

Wizardry & Wild Romance represents one of Moorcock's expeditions to expand the world, and readers' understanding of it. As with all of Moorcock's efforts, it is an act of generosity. *Wizardry* rewards, as they say, repeated re-reading. MonkeyBrain Books should be commended for bringing it back into print. And you should acquire enough copies to send to anyone you know who cares about fantasy, epic or otherwise.

INDEX

ABOUT THE AUTHOR

Born shortly after the beginning of WW2, Michael Moorcock's earliest memories are of a blitzed London. His neighborhood experienced the V-bombs particularly badly and he believes that his penchant for visualising warped and altered landscapes has something to do with the fact that every day he left his house the landscape had changed. Growing up in London, he knew the city as a zone of destruction around St Paul's Cathedral and some of the other older buildings. It was easy for him to imagine what old London must have been like. His earliest reading consisted of the family books (Edgar Rice Burroughs, George Bernard Shaw, Edward Lester Arnold – he jokes that he thought all authors had to have at least three names, which is why he included his middle name or initial in his earliest work) and whatever he could borrow from the local commercial lending library. "It was a goldmine of popular fiction," he says, "from detective thrillers to science fiction, from Ruby M. Ayres to P.G.Wodehouse." Later the public library gave him Aldous Huxley, H.G.Wells, Mervyn Peake, Virginia Woolf and Angus Wilson. He also had a particular fascination for the popular magazines produced before he was born. He still has an extensive collection of British magazines like *Pearson's*, *The Strand* and *Lilliput*, as well as a large collection of *Argosy* and other American popular short story magazines of their day. For several years he sent off to dealers, buying the weekly adventure story magazines like *Magnet*, *Thriller* and *Union Jack* some thirty years after they had appeared, purchasing each number by the week for the week it originally appeared in so that he could follow the serials and series. He next discovered American sf pulps in the English second hand bookstores and was soon a keen reader of *Planet* and *Startling Stories*. His longest lasting favourite character from those early days is Zenith the Albino, an adversary of the world's second greatest detective Sexton Blake, whose adventures had been appearing since the 1890s. He based his character Elric of Melnibone on Zenith and has written a number of homages to Blake and Zenith. As a boy he published many fanzines, such as *Outlaws Own*, and edited his first professional magazine at the age of 16, *Tarzan Adventures*, to which he introduced a mixture of text stories and comics. In the 1960s he worked as an editor and contributor to Sexton Blake Library, also producing dozens of stories of Robin Hood, Dick Turpin, Buffalo Bill, Kit Carson, Buck Jones, Dogfight Dixon, RFC. and Karl the Viking both as text and as comics. He got an early start, he says, in the folk hero business. Meanwhile he was making his reputation in the British SF magazines and elsewhere, most famously with his character Elric. By 1964 he had taken over editorship of *New Worlds Science Fiction* which became the chief publication of what later was known as the SF "New Wave." *New Worlds* got into trouble with government and retailers for using what at the time were considered "tabu" stories and ideas. In this, Moorcock, thinks, the magazine had more in common with *Evergreen Review* than with sf magazines. He was more interested in finding literary forms which could cope with modern subjects in a way which modernism could not. Sf, rooted in popular forms but dealing with intellectual ideas, seemed the ideal place to start. In this sense *New Worlds* was probably the first post-modernist magazine. *New Worlds* was a hugely influential magazine in Britain, as much on the general cultural world as upon the world of sf. Winning several major prizes for his fiction through the sixties and seventies, Moorcock eventually gave up editing and increasingly concentrated on his fiction, much of which remained literary rather than generic. In the eighties he published *Byzantium Endures* and *The Laughter of Carthage*, two in a sequence of four novels attempting to find the roots of the Nazi Holocaust through the eyes of the unreliable and despicable, but somehow likeable, con-man Colonel Pyat. *Mother London*, a celebration of his home city, was short-listed (with Rushdie's *Satanic Verses* and Chatwyn's *Utz*) for the 1988 Whitbread Prize, Britain's most prestigious literary award. As well as publishing further literary novels, including *Jerusalem Commands* and *King of the City*, Moorcock has also published more Elric adventures beginning with *The Dreamthief's Daughter* and a series of homages including *Lost Sorceress of the Silent Citadel* (homage to Leigh Brackett), and *The Affair of the Texan's Honour* (homage to Conan Doyle). Seaton Begg stories can be found in his collection *Fabulous Harbors* and in *McSweeney's Magazine*. These include *The Affair of the Seven Virgins* and *The Case of the Nazi Canary*. He has also returned to his famous Jerry Cornelius character, the most recent being the novella *Firing the Cathedral*. *The Lives and Times of Jerry Cornelius*, containing these recent stories, was published in Fall 2003. Having recently completed the final volume in the Colonel Pyat sequence, *The Vengeance of Rome*, he is working on an Elric graphic novel for DC Comics with Walter Simonson, as well as his final Elric novel *The White Wolf's Son*. He contributes journalism regularly to *The Guardian*, *The Spectator* and others. Moorcock has been married three times, currently to his long-time spouse Linda Steele, and has three children (Sophie, Katherine and Max) by his first wife the novelist Hilary Bailey, two grandchildren and more on the way. He and his wife have homes in Spain and Texas and spend long periods in England.